HIPPO GHOST

The Ghost Twin

Richard Brown

To Sylvia

Scholastic Children's Books,
Commonwealth House,
1-19 New Oxford Street,
London WC1A 1NU, UK
A division of Scholastic Ltd
London ~ New York ~ Toronto ~ Sydney ~ Auckland

First published in the UK by Scholastic Ltd, 1998

Copyright © Richard Brown, 1998

ISBN 0 590 11236 8

Typeset by
Cambrian Typesetters, Frimley, Camberley, Surrey
Printed by
Mackays of Chatham PLC, Chatham, Kent

10 9 8 7 6 5 4 3 2 1

Chapter 1

Now was the time to do it. It was Sunday afternoon. Dad was in the study, working on the computer, Mum was dozing on a lounger in the conservatory, listening to the radio. The perfect time for James to slip away. *Going out to play. Back for tea*, he scribbled on a piece of paper. But he wasn't going out to play, far from it. What he was about to do made his heart thump uncomfortably and his hand shake as he quietly closed the front door.

James hurried down street after street, keeping his head down.

He came at last to the *cul de sac* that led to the old block of flats. Here he leaned against the road sign to catch his breath. The road was deserted except for a man cleaning a car. A cat on a windowsill nearby peered at him suspiciously through slit eyes. The sun slid behind a cloud, like a curtain being closed over a window. James shivered.

I can't do it, he said to himself. *I can't*. After all, it was only a dream. A dream of Joe. He'd had plenty of such dreams over the years. But *this* one was different. Joe had been so alive, so vivid, so real. Not the pale shadow on his heart that he had become, not like a character in a book, felt rather than seen, but *someone alive*. Joe was calling to him. *Come back home*, the voice in his head said over and over again.

So James was going back home. What was once home. The place where his twin brother had been killed three years ago.

He felt he was walking on air: the pressure of every footstep was cushioned by fear, anticipation, longing. The block of flats loomed at the end of the road.

The metal frets of the barrier set around the flats felt cold against the skin of his cheek. *Demolition site. For your own safety, keep out*, said the sign above his head. But the paint on it was already flaking. "When will they ever get round to pulling it down?" he heard the echo of his father say. He knew how much Dad looked forward to the day when no trace of that block of flats existed any more. The windows were boarded up, the ground was choked with rubbish, tall grass and weeds stirred in the breeze.

James stared at one particular window on the fifth floor. *That used to be my room*, he said to himself, *mine and Joe's*. He caught a sudden memory: he and Joe dropping from that window toy soldiers on handkerchief parachutes which Dad had made for them, Mum patiently catching them below and collecting them up. He swallowed hard and turned away. The street yawned emptily ahead of him. He couldn't go back.

He worked his way through scratching weeds until he found a gap in the fence at the back. Other people had squeezed through here, perhaps vagrants looking for somewhere to sleep, or kids using it as a playground. There were tracks in the vegetation, wending their way to the building. Wood panelling had been prised away from one ground-floor window. James listened fearfully by that window, afraid that someone might be lurking the other side of it, waiting to seize him as he entered. But it was silent. He peered into the dark interior; a pungent, dank smell hit him and he turned back, gasping for breath.

He couldn't do it. His legs felt too weak, his breath came in fits and starts. He wanted to be at home, in his room, reading his book: there was excitement enough in that for him. But even as he put his first foot forward, he heard a voice whispering hoarsely in his head: *Don't be a coward, James. Don't leave me here. You've got to come.*

Fearfully, James pushed open the flat door; someone had broken the lock. The hall was lit by light from open doors. James stared at the pattern on the faded hall carpet. It bought back a flood of memories: he and Joe shooting cars up and down the hall, racing to see who could get to their coat first (the coat pegs were still there on the wall...)

Standing in the hall, where the light criss-crossed from the lounge and his parents' bedroom, James called out, "Joe?" His voice had to force itself past a lump in his throat. He expected the silence, but he sensed something or someone was watching him. Warily he peered into each room as he passed. Dust, paint flakes, peeling wallpaper, a few bits of abandoned furniture, some bottles left on the sill – that was all. Faded, airless, and sad.

Slowly – leaving it till last – James pushed open the door of the bedroom he had once shared with his twin brother. Strangely, there were curtains still up at the windows – he recognized the pattern of helicopters, hot-air balloons and aeroplanes on them – and the room was stuffy, in shadow. He stepped in warily, his heart beating so fast there was a kind of drumming sound in his ears.

"Joe?" His voice sounded cracked. He swallowed hard, took a deep breath, and echoed the name. "Joe?"

Nothing.

All at once he felt, how silly to be standing there, calling the name of his dead brother in the dark!

He peered out of the grimy window. Nothing had changed out there: the trees, the roofscape, the insect-like traffic crawling along the quiet streets, the glitter of the river in the distant park. It was comforting to keep his eyes on that. Behind him, in the room in which he had spent the first few happy years of his life with Joe, memories stirred.

They were in the lift on the fourth floor, waiting to go down. Mum had already pressed the button, when Joe suddenly dodged out of the lift and shouted, "I'll race you down."

"No, Joe, come back," Mum called, but it was already too late. The doors closed on James and Mum, leaving Joe outside. That was the last time James saw his twin brother alive. Someone above had already pressed the button for the lift: they had to go up before they could go down again. When they reached the ground floor, it was already too late. Joe had raced down the

*stairs in his usual impetuous way, determined
to be first. At the bottom he continued running
through the open door, and the force of his
flight had propelled him straight into the path
of an accelerating blue van. He bounced off
the side of it. He might have been all right if
he hadn't been thrown against a concrete
bollard and cracked his head. When Mum and
James came out into the sunlight, his body was
still.*

Suddenly, James felt cold air on the back of
his head. Slowly, stiffening with fear, he
turned his head.

In the corner of the room, where their
bunk bed used to be, there was a soft, blueish
light. No more than a mist at first, it grew
brighter and denser by the second. It
shimmered and swirled until it settled into
the shape of a human. A boy.

Joe!

James was shaking all over. He had never
felt so cold. He wanted to flee the place. But
he couldn't move.

Joe's face formed out of the mist. His eyes

glittered a greenish blue and glowed like a cat's in the dark. His body was white, insubstantial, naked at first, but soon took on colour and then clothes – a wavering image of the same clothes that James was wearing. After what seemed an ageless time for James, the ghost of his dead twin brother was standing before him, hovering just above the floor.

Joe was the same age as himself. In his dreams, as time passed, Joe's image had grown more and more vague, undefined, as if he was slowly slipping away into nothingness. Now he saw Joe in every detail – Joe and himself, for they were so identical he could almost be looking at his mirror image. It was only the paleness of the skin and the luminous eyes that marked out the living from the dead. That and the defiance of gravity.

Joe grinned at him, then pointed and laughed.

Took your time, didn't you? said a voice in his head. Joe's voice. So like his own. *I've been calling for you for ages!* He laughed again, softer now, a note of relief in his voice. *I was always racing ahead of you, remember? While you held on to Mum's hand. What kept you?*

James tried to say something but his mouth was so dry, his throat so tight, nothing came out.

Are you frightened of me? Joe shimmered slightly, as if the thought amused him. *Don't be. We're brothers. Twins. I am part of you, remember? You are part of me.*

They stared at each other. The cold luminosity of Joe's eyes softened and James broke away from the ghost's hypnotic gaze. He fixed his eyes on the wording on Joe's sweatshirt, *St Joseph's*, the name of his primary school: if this was a mirror image, the writing should be reversed, he thought.

But it isn't, is it? Joe grinned.

James, startled, looked back into Joe's eyes.

You don't need to say anything, said Joe in his head. *We can telepathize. Don't you remember, we could always do that?*

Remember? Since birth they had lived in each other's thoughts, anticipated each other's wishes, knew what each other was feeling. It was so much a part of their existence, James thought it was the most natural thing in the world. Only after he had lost it did he know how precious it was. It was the thing he missed most of all after Joe's death, that voice inside his head. Now, hearing it again, he felt something hard and cold, like an icicle in his chest, shudder, crack and melt away. He wanted to cry, but he held the feeling in and smiled instead.

Plucking up courage, he asked, *Are you – a ghost, then?*

Joe smiled, as if it was a huge joke. *But you mustn't be afraid of me. I'm still your brother. Remember that – always.*

James stared at him intensely, trying to make sense of this fact. Suddenly, he felt a warmth begin to flow through him; he stopped trembling. "I've missed you, Joe," he whispered.

Me too. How many times have I wished you were a ghost too? He laughed again. Then his voice changed. *No, I didn't mean that. Being a ghost is horrible.*

How strange it was to hear that voice again. *If you've been like this, I mean, a ghost ever since... Why has it taken so long for me to find you?*

Joe shrugged. *Time means little to a ghost — didn't you know that? Where ghosts live — where I live, although you can't call it living...* He paused; his body flickered light. *You drift in nothingness, like space without stars; and when you return to earth, you find weeks, months, years have passed. Out there, a week can seem like a year, or a month like a day. It's all different, there's no real time. To me it seems like only yesterday I bounced off that van and cracked my head; but it can seem like a century ago.*

But you're here now. I've been dreaming about you lately, hearing your voice again. Why now?

I've been trying extra hard to get through to you. I've missed you so much too. That's what's kept me here, kept me coming back instead of drifting away for ever. I've been calling for you to come these last few days. I didn't know where you were. I was frightened that you might have moved far away.

Tentatively, James reached out a hand to touch Joe. He wanted some reassurance that he wasn't just imagining all this.

No, don't, said Joe, shrinking back. *We should not touch. Not yet.*

James's hand fell away; he felt disappointed.

There was a silence.

It was only when I saw the flat again, said James. *With Dad. And something told me you – your ghost – that you were still here. My dreams kept telling me to come back. I would have come earlier if I'd known.*

Joe sighed, and a thin curl of mist came out of his mouth. *You came just in time. They're going to knock this block of flats down. Soon, I know it. I shall have nowhere to go. This is my home, see? My haunt. Every ghost has to have their haunt, otherwise they can't come back.* Suddenly, Joe's eyes dimmed, his shoulders hunched; he looked frightened.

You'll be all right, said James. *This place has been derelict for years. Why should they knock it down now? I'll come and see you as often as I can.*

Joe shook his head. *It's going to happen soon, James, you'll see.*

He turned away. James watched him climb into what he knew to be the lower bunk bed, although he could not see it. He watched Joe curl up on the bed, his body, now horizontal, seeming to hover a metre or so above the floor. *Take me with you, James. Please.*

A prickly excitement made James pace up and down the room. What had he wished for all these years since his brother's death, deep down inside himself? That his brother should suddenly be there, there by his side where he belonged, *always*. It had been a cry in the dark, shut away from the world because it hurt so much. Now the door was opening, the deep wish was coming true. James felt the excitement bubble up until he was ready to burst. He leapt towards the ghost of his brother...

No, don't!

But it was too late. Joe held up his hand to try and ward him off. Their hands touched. Then sprang apart. Between their fingers a sudden, sizzling current of blue light formed. It glowed fiercely, luminously between them. Joe sat up. Suddenly, his eyes were glowing brightly again, and colour suffused his pale skin. By contrast, James felt weak. Light dimmed in his eyes, his knees buckled, he crumpled to the floor. As he fell, the contact was broken and the current between them faded.

I tried to tell you, said Joe.

What happened? said James, getting up slowly off the floor, bewildered.

Energy passed between us, Joe said excitedly. *The energy of the living. Or rather, from you to me. It's happened once or twice before, with strangers. It's dangerous, I think. For you. But perhaps also for me. I gain a weird kind of strength from it. It makes me want to live again.* He got up off the invisible bed. *That's not good for a ghost, is it?*

James brushed the dust off his jeans and hands. He felt strangely weak. *Why not?* he asked.

Because... Because... Ghosts feed on energy left over from their former lives. It's the energy of unfinished business – you know, things that had to be done in life before... Joe shrugged. *But I don't know.*

Joe's voice faded into uncertainty. James didn't know what he was talking about. He wiped his brow. *I felt really weak then. As if I was about to faint.*

I felt just the opposite. I felt alive. You cannot understand what that means to a ghost.

I'm sorry, said James, instinctively reaching out.

Joe shrank back. *We* must *keep our distance*, he said. *As long as we don't touch, we'll be all right.*

OK, said James. He didn't know what else to say. He still felt weak. He went back to the window, as to a familiar place, and peered out. How strange the world now looked, unreal, sealed behind glass, silent.

Presently, Joe joined him there. He was careful to keep a metre or so of space between them. Peering down, he said, *Remember the parachutes?*

Those words cut right through James. He buried his face in his arms and with unexpected force he began to sob.

Joe stood by helpless, his eyes flickering, his skin faintly luminous in the shadow. He was thinking, *I wish I could hold him, tell him everything's all right. Everything will be all right in the end. Now that we're together again.* But he could only watch his brother's shoulders heave and listen to his brother's convulsions.

But although there were years of sorrow in James's tears, there was an enormous feeling of relief too. He had found his brother again.

When his tears had gone, he turned to Joe and said with sudden excitement, *Do you really want to stay here?*

Not any more.

Then come home with me.

Your home?

Yes. What's yours is mine. We always said that, remember?

The ghost of Joe smiled. *I knew you were going to say that.*

James turned towards the door. *Just follow me, then.*

Wait.

What's the matter?

I'm a ghost, remember? No one must see me. You must understand that.

James's face fell. *But you must...* he began. Then stopped. Joe was grinning.

There are some advantages in being a ghost, he said. *For one thing, you can change shape and size. Watch this.*

Joe's body began to lose its shape. Within a few seconds he had lost his outline, his facial features dissolved, his clothes faded. He became a ball which shrank and shrank until it was no larger than a tennis ball. It hovered in front of James, a little glowing sphere of pale light.

Now it's safe to touch me, said Joe. *I'm holding all my cold energy in a tight ball: none of it can escape when I'm like this. Cup me in the palms of your hand.*

The ball of light that was Joe, or Joe's spirit, settled into his brother's hands. It felt very cold, like a snowball, yet it had no weight.

James carried him gingerly down the stairs. He paused in the entrance. *Can you be any shape you want?* he asked.

I can be a ball of light. I can be invisible too, although that takes up much more energy and makes me tired. I can look like my old self, too, but I'm not sure what else I can be. Now, can we get moving?

James carried his brother all the way home. People who saw him pass wondered what he had in his hands, for they could see nothing there except for a pale, mysterious light. *If only they knew*, he thought, a sharp excitement running through him.

If only they knew, repeated his brother. James felt his laugh echo inside him.

Chapter 2

A few days before that momentous event in the deserted flat, James had had a birthday party. Or rather, a birthday tea, since only he and his parents were present.

James was well aware that boys of his age had long ago grown out of birthday teas or parties, and he was ashamed of the fact that his parents – his mother in particular – insisted on continuing with them. But he knew why. The party wasn't just for him, it was for Joe too. The memory of Joe. But of course no one said so. James would much rather have had a meal in McDonalds followed by a good science-fiction movie at the cinema, but he knew better than to suggest it.

"Who are you going to invite to your party?" Mum asked him.

He knew she only asked out of politeness. If he'd suggested anyone, she would have found some way of dissuading them. He would have liked to have asked his friend Johnno, big, owlish Johnno who always had his head buried in a book on stars and planets. If Johnno came, he'd never notice anything was odd. Or Zena: she'd go to anyone's party. She was so bright, bubbly, noisy, everyone soon got tired of her, everyone except James, for she did all the talking for both of them. But no, he knew it was better not to ask.

He did say, "Do we have to have a party?" but Mum's pursed lips and stiffening shoulders were answer enough, and he turned away from her before she had time to say anything. He'd tried getting Dad to break the habit and take him out on his birthday, but Dad had just shaken his head and said, "I wouldn't mind, James, but your mother wouldn't like it. She sets great store by these birthday parties, you know that. Just try and enjoy it, OK?"

He even knew what present he would be given. What he really wanted was a pair of roller-blades. He'd seen kids zooming along the high street in little packs, swerving from side to side as they made their swift, silent progress, and nothing seemed more desirable to him than to join a gang like that and move with such speed. But it was dangerous – or so his mum would think. His dad too, perhaps. And anything remotely dangerous sent a shudder through his tight little family.

No, he'd have to make do with a watch. He'd been with Dad to the market and had seen on a stall a glittering, complicated-looking watch which had several dials giving times in different time zones. That would do, he thought with a sigh, that would be a *safe* present. He pointed it out to Dad and then purposely turned away to look at some books on a neighbouring stall to give Dad the chance to buy it. Out of the corner of his eye, he watched Dad hand over the money. Well, at least *that* problem was solved.

Joe's death had curtailed James's freedom in many ways. For example, he was usually driven to school, even though it was only about a mile away on a perfectly safe route. He was seldom allowed out on his own. Rough sports like football were discouraged. Climbing trees was banned. If James had been the rebellious sort, he would have soon broken all these rules. But he wasn't, he was timid, and he knew it.

At least the watch was admired at school.

After registration, Mrs McNab, his teacher, announced brightly that it was his birthday, and he had to stand before the class and tell them about the watch. He blushed and mumbled and they told him to speak up; then he got his explanation of different time zones muddled so that everyone laughed. But it was a good-natured laugh and he didn't really mind.

Johnno and Zena stayed in with him at break and lunchtime. Johnno was excited about a meteorite that was about to sail past planet Earth and would be visible at night to the naked eye. Zena was full of an aunt's wedding. Together, they filled up the silence around him and kept him amused. That was always how it was: they seldom asked him what he was thinking, it was as if they expected nothing more from him than a listening ear.

Mrs McNab knew his mother: they had been at school together. She knew all about Joe too.

"How was your mum this morning?" she asked James.

James knew what was behind the question, but how could he tell? Mum had been a bit pale, her eyes were a bit red, but she'd smiled and given him a brief, unexpected hug before he left the car. "All right," he mumbled.

"Are you having a party?"

James nodded.

Mrs McNab knew by that nod just what James thought of his party. She sighed. "You do understand?" she said, her head to one side.

He nodded warily; he understood all right.

"I must give your mum a ring," Mrs McNab added. "It's a long time since we had a good chat. Tell her for me, will you?"

Mum worked part-time in a library, but she had taken the day off work, as she always did on James's birthday. She had shopped and baked all day, creating a spread of food far more substantial than the three of them could possibly eat. For days after, they would live on half-eaten jellies, drying sausage rolls, pungent-smelling boiled eggs and chunks of assorted cakes.

James was allowed to walk home that day. When he arrived home, he dropped his bag in the hall and went straight to the dining-room. A magnificent spread met his eyes. On a green tablecloth, gaudy crackers, red serviettes and glittering glasses set off the mounds of food, the jellies, cakes, sandwiches, pies; it was a sight that always thrilled him, like a vision from some fairy-tale past. He let his gaze linger on the sight –

but skirted the space in the middle of the table. That was reserved for the birthday cake which Mum always brought in at the end of the meal, blazing with candles.

"Well?" said Mum.

"It's great," he said, and there was such genuine pleasure in his eyes, Mum smiled.

"I just wish..." he murmured in spite of himself.

There was a little silence. "Yes?"

"Oh, nothing," he murmured.

"No, go on, you can say it."

"Well, I just wish Johnno and Zena could have come."

"You should have asked them," she said. He looked at her in surprise: did she really mean it?

"Never mind. We'll have a good time, anyway."

She gestured to a few more wrapped presents set by his place at the table. "You can open those now, if you like. There's one from Grandad, and one from Uncle Terry. And some extras from us."

"Where's Dad?" he asked.

"He'll be a little late, I'm afraid. He rang just before you came in."

"I'll open my presents when he's here," said James.

"Just as you like. I've got a few things to do in the kitchen. Put the television on until Dad gets here."

But he didn't. As soon as she had gone, he stared at the table again. There were *four places*. That was so normal for his birthday party – his and Joe's birthday party – he'd hardly noticed it at first. He sat in his own chair and looked across at the empty one that was Joe's.

A sudden longing for his twin curled up from his stomach into his throat. "I wish you *were* here," he said to himself. It felt so lonely in that room, all on his own. He leaned back in his chair, half-closing his eyes.

The tick of the clock on the mantelpiece seemed to get louder, slower, soporific. And then Joe's image formed out of the streaks of light and shadow between his eyelashes. That haunting face: thick, black hair, wide, lustrous blue eyes, a broad mouth, a sense of daring. He was holding out a cracker and saying, *Go on, James, pull this one with me*. James reached across and grasped the cracker, and then they pulled and pulled, as in a tussle of strength, but the cracker would not break. They pulled harder. All of a sudden there was a bang, and they reeled back. Something fell out of the cracker. Peering down at it, they saw it was a tiny blue plastic van. James gasped and looked up at Joe, but Joe was already fading.

"No," James shouted. "Come back, Joe, come back."

Mum rushed in. She saw the bewilderment, the anguish, on his face. "What's the matter?" she said. "You were making such a strange noise."

"I saw him. Joe. He was there." He pointed with a trembling finger at Joe's chair.

"Oh, James," Mum murmured. She stared at the chair too. "You mustn't say that. Oh, but it's my fault, I..."

"He was my age, Mum," James butted in, a sudden truth dawning in his face. "Not a little kid. My age. It's *his* birthday too, you see."

His mother left the room, her hand to her mouth. James knew better than to follow her. How stupid of him to upset her on this of all days.

Dad arrived home half an hour later. "Sorry, son," he said, flinging down his briefcase in a gesture of disgust and taking off his jacket. "Meetings! The bane of my life. How's my birthday boy, then?"

James immediately cheered up; with Dad there, the brittle silence of the house was broken.

James opened his presents in front of his parents. He got a compass set from his grandfather and a football album from his uncle, neither of which particularly interested him. There was a calculator from Dad and a writing-set from Mum. He placed around the table the birthday cards he had got from some of his classmates, giving pride of place to those from Johnno and Zena. Then they ate. James and Dad made sure that they tried everything. Mum nibbled here and there.

All three were conscious of the empty place at the table. Usually, at some point in the birthday meal, Joe's memory would be evoked. Dad would raise his glass of squash and would say something like, "To Joe, who remains with us," and Mum would add something like, "Always," or "In our hearts." James was not expected to add anything; indeed, he would have been too tongue-tied, for his parents' words embarrassed him. This time, nothing was said. When it was time for the cake to be brought in, Dad went into the kitchen with Mum. He heard them arguing about something in low, urgent tones. While he waited, he picked up a cracker and tried to pull it himself in his two hands, but was surprised to find that he couldn't: he only succeeded in crumpling it. This made him despair and he threw the cracker aside in disgust.

Mum brought in the cake, a circle of candles flickering above the white icing. Dad followed, a slightly strained look on his face. Mum placed the cake in the centre of the table. James saw at once what the argument had been about. The writing on the cake had always said, *Happy Birthday, James and Joe*. Now it said, *Happy Birthday, James*, followed by a smear in the icing where Joe's name had been.

James pretended not to notice. But he had to force the cake down.

Dad showed clear relief that the meal was over. He produced a small package from his briefcase. "Now, then, my lad," he said with forced cheerfulness. "I'm going to make an ornithologist of you yet. See this?" He held up the package. "It's an extra present. Here."

It turned out to be a CD-Rom on bird identification. James smiled. For years Dad had been trying to get him to identify the birds that came to their bird-table in the garden. He'd taken James on trips to rivers, lakes, gravel pits and the like, with binoculars and guide books, intent on imparting to the boy his passion for birds. James had liked the attention, and had tried hard in his way to remember how one set of feathers differed from another, but he had felt no kindling of interest and his memory always let him down.

"Come upstairs," said Dad. "See what you make of it."

Later, in his pyjamas, James went into his parents' bedroom, prompted by Dad to say thank you to Mum for the party.

He found her sitting on the bed surrounded by photographs. There was a sad, quiet look about her face, but James sensed a sort of happiness underneath it and he decided to linger.

"Thanks for the party, Mum," he said.

She smiled and patted the bed beside her.

"What are you doing?" he said, settling beside her and picking up a photograph of the three of them, taken last year in Wales on holiday.

"I bought a new photograph album today. It's big enough to take all these photographs. I haven't sorted any of them since..." But she wouldn't say it. She had no need to James had spent many hours looking through the albums she'd kept when they were a family of four. But there had been no albums of them as a family of three; the photographs had remained unsorted in their numerous packages.

"That's great, Mum. Can I help you?"

"I don't know where to start."

"Let's put all the holidays together."

James spent a rare and happy hour with his mother, recalling so much of their shared past.

"Remember that?" she would say. "When you were too frightened to go into the sea, and Dad had to carry you in. How you screamed!"

James nodded. But what he remembered more clearly was how fearlessly Joe took to the water, splashing about in the waves, laughing when knocked over by the surge of water. Joe could swim almost before he could walk. James had never learnt to.

Or, "Oh, look at this. That big fish Dad caught.He was so proud of that and you went and flung it back in the river before he could weigh it. We didn't know whether to laugh or cry."

James took the photograph and smiled. He recalled the look of sheer panic in the fish's eye. And his dad's tight-lipped silence on their way home that day.

Many of the photographs were hard to place, and eventually they had to call Dad away from his computer to help them.

It was late, but as they sat around the bed together, they were able to reduce the scatter of photographs of their lives together into neat little piles.

"Where's the new album, Mum?" James asked.

Looking back on that night, he wished he'd never asked that question, innocent as it was.

"We won't start putting them in it tonight," Mum said. "It's far too late."

"I just wanted to see it."

"OK, I'll get it. Then it's time for your bed, young man, birthday or no birthday."

She left to fetch the album.

Dad shifted uncomfortably on the bed.

"Mum said something to me earlier," he said. "She told me that you saw something in the dining-room." He looked embarrassed.

James nodded, blushing suddenly. He didn't want to talk about this.

"What did you see?" There was a sudden urgency in his voice which made James sit up.

"I saw Joe. We were pulling a cracker together. And when it went bang..." But he couldn't go on.

"Tell me," Dad urged, taking his son's shoulder and shaking him slightly. "Too much is bottled up in this house already."

James looked into his dad's narrowed eyes. "A little blue plastic van fell out. That's all."

Dad let go of his shoulder and looked away. "You didn't tell Mum that, did you?" he said quietly.

"I wouldn't dare," said James, trying to make a joke of it.

"Good lad," Dad said, patting his son's shoulder.

Then they were aware that Mum was standing in the doorway. They did not know how much she had heard. But the look of hurt, of fury almost, on her face, told them that she had heard enough. Her reaction was extraordinary. She had a big red photo album in her hands. She raised it and hurled it at Dad, hitting him painfully on the arm.

"You can put the pictures in that yourself," she shouted. "I don't want anything more to do with it."

They heard her lock herself in the bathroom.

They sat there, stunned.

"Go to bed now, son," Dad said quietly.

That night James had the first of the really vivid dreams about Joe. So vivid, it seemed that Joe was there in the bedroom beside him when he woke in the dark and called out his brother's name. "Why don't you leave us alone," he muttered to himself; but he didn't mean it. He knew, as he settled down to sleep again, that if he did stop thinking and dreaming of his twin brother each day, something would have died inside him too.

Chapter 3

James got up very early the next day. His head was still full of images of Joe. Solid images. Joe older, just like himself. Joe *calling to him*. He pulled open the curtains in the dining-room. On the table were his birthday cards in a neat little pile: had his party only been yesterday? It seemed an age ago already.

He saw the row of photograph albums in the bookcase and knew then what had prompted him to come down so early, and to come in here first.

He sat at the table and slowly turned page after page of each album... He and Joe as babies in a pram, his mother leaning over and smiling proudly. The nurse holding them. Dad with one of them on each knee...

Joe holding a hose pipe in the garden, spraying a cowering James with cold water. Joe sitting in the dog kennel, hugging Sheba, the dog Mum could never bear to replace. Joe zooming down the playground slide, shrieking his delight, while James, afraid of heights, screamed his refusal to go up. Joe winning the running race at their first sports day. Joe holding up his first swimming certificate... James turned the page. There was Joe in his first Nativity play, stealing the show with his loud voice and winning smirk...

And so it went on.

James never felt jealous. He was content to enjoy Joe's successes from the sidelines. It was as if Joe was doing it for them both. And he knew instinctively that without his twin brother's silent inner strength to come back to, Joe would never have had the courage to do all these things so boldly, so confidently. But others did not see it that way: certainly not his parents. Mum was always sighing over James's inactivity, making excuses for him, being too protective. Dad was always urging him to have a go, to join in, to be like his brother. They did not understand that beneath the brothers' physical likeness, there were different personalities: one outgoing, one inward-looking. It seemed natural to the twins: why couldn't others see it that way?

James turned another page. Here there was just one, enlarged photograph, taken perhaps a year before Joe's death. The boys, in their summer shorts and T-shirts, were sitting side by side on the patio step in the garden. They had a large picture book between them. James was teaching Joe to read. He closed his eyes and relived that little scene. Reading had come easy to James: the squiggles beneath the pictures soon became a voice telling him a story in his head. But not to Joe. He squirmed, he wriggled, he slapped the book, giggled over the pictures, pulled at the pages, started at the end or in the middle, threw it aside, trampled on it – anything but actually look at the words. His parents, his first teachers, despaired. Only James could get him to point at the words, to say them, to repeat them, to string them at last into sentences. As he took that picture, Dad had no idea that he was recording a breakthrough: the first time Joe had really begun to read. The story had been about a little monster who found a boy under his bed and was scared stiff of it. Joe soon knew that story off by heart. "I'm the monster," he'd say, "and you're the boy." But then another day he'd change his mind, it was the other way round; James didn't mind.

"I thought I heard you come down," said Dad in a puzzled voice. "What are you doing?"

James gestured to the albums.

"Oh, James," Dad sighed. "You mustn't let last night upset you."

James shook his head.

He pushed towards Dad a photograph of Joe winning a fancy dress prize dressed up as a space monster. Dad chuckled. "I remember that," he said. "It drove your mother to despair, making that mask. What did you wear that day?"

"I didn't," James mumbled.

"You wouldn't, I remember. Mum wasn't pleased."

"We are very different, you know," said James with sudden defiance.

Dad looked at him quizzically. "*Were*, James. Not *are*," he said quietly, moving away from the table. "Now pack up those albums and come and help me get breakfast. Mum's got a headache and won't be down. You'll have to walk to school today, OK? I've got to leave early. So buck up, right?"

All the way to school James imagined Joe walking in step beside him. Or sometimes skipping ahead, kicking a stone, cavorting about, making faces, then falling into step again. Inside his head, they talked, about friends, teachers, school work, kids they didn't like; they cracked jokes, boasted, revealed absurd wishes, laughed at nothing, shared fears; and always with perfect understanding. It was hard to do this when

Mum drove him to school in the car and picked him up after school. That was why he loved these rare walks to school on his own, why he walked so slowly, so thoughtfully, stretching it out until the last possible moment before he entered the playground. In quiet reading or writing times, too, he could imagine Joe beside him; but it was always harder to do that with other people around.

"So what film did you see?" Zena asked him as they came out of assembly.

"I didn't," he admitted.

"So you had a party after all?" said Johnno, preparing to be annoyed that he wasn't invited.

James shook his head.

His friends looked at each other; they understood. Weird parents.

It wasn't a lie, he thought, it was hardly a party. Not a real one. He felt ashamed.

"How was it?" Mrs McNab asked him in little more than a whisper. He was changing for gym; he managed to hide his embarrassment by pulling his T-shirt over his head. "OK," he said. "We had plenty of food."

"Did you give your mum my message?"

"No, I forgot. I'm sorry."

Mrs McNab tutted. "You'll forget your own head one day, James," she said with a smile.

"He often does already," said Zena, tying up her hair.

"But you'd never notice," said Johnno.

Gym, as usual for James, was a nightmare. His body refused to roll over on the mat, it got dizzy at the top of the climbing frame, it baulked at the horse, it wobbled on the bench, it rolled off the mats at crazy angles. Zena found all this hilarious and had to be shushed by a patient Mrs McNab. Johnno ignored him, knowing that he was beyond help. The rest of the class put him down as useless. There was always one in every class.

He was able to pull his scattered self together during the next period, when Mrs McNab read to them from a book about the Victorians. While the others followed what she was reading in the textbook, James was already well ahead: he'd never had any trouble reading.

Writing was the problem. Having to remember every letter in every word, and at the same time to control the movement of his hand to form each letter and join them correctly, proved too much for him. He was terrified of getting his spellings wrong. As a result, he wrote very little, and what he did write was spidery, full of rubbings out, covered in smudges. It puzzled everyone except himself. Joe had been just the opposite: he would never settle to reading on his own; but when an idea seized him, he could dash down pages and pages of writing, to the delight of his teacher. That puzzled everyone even more, for weren't identical twins supposed to be, well, identical in everything they did?

He liked history and English – as long as it didn't involve writing – and he was good at making up short poems when it was his turn for the computer. But not art: he had plenty of ideas, plenty of vivid pictures and patterns in his mind, but his hands were too clumsy, and what emerged was a horrible travesty.

Mrs McNab made allowances for him, but she secretly despaired. "He's a bright lad," she said to his parents. "It's just that something goes wrong whenever he tries to put his ideas down on paper." His parents were used by now to hearing this; they no longer nagged him about it or tried to help him at home. Mrs McNab had consulted James's records. She noted from the early samples of his work that he had been progressing well, but after Joe's death, he had fallen further and further behind. *Intelligent*, it said, *but lacks confidence. Needs time to get over his brother's death.* But how much time? Would he ever get over it?

"Now, class," Mrs McNab said, picking up and opening a book.

They had packed up a good hour earlier than expected. Another hour and the weekend would start, and next week was the autumn half-term holiday. They all felt excited and impatient.

"Settle down, Zena. Don't you ever stop?"

"No, Miss," Zena retorted with a grin.

Mrs McNab sighed and cleared her throat.

"As you know, Class Six always puts on a Christmas play. It's your chance to shine. Now, Christmas may seem a long way away at the moment..."

"What are we going to do?" Zena butted in.

"Hands up, Zena."

She put her hand up and was made to ask again.

Mrs McNab held up the book. "*A Christmas Carol* by Charles Dickens. Anyone ever heard of it? Read it?"

A few hands went up.

"I saw a pantomime of it once," someone said.

"I've read the Ladybird version," said another.

"Well, this is the real thing," said Mrs McNab. "Does anyone know the story?"

James found himself saying, "Aren't there ghosts in it?" He spoke in a chance moment of silence and because he so seldom volunteered anything in class, everyone turned to look at him.

"That's right, James. Do you know anything more about the story?"

He shook his head. He thought he did, but with everyone watching, he hadn't the courage to say any more.

"Let me tell you something of it, then," Mrs NcNab said to the class. "It's set in the middle of the last century, I think, at Christmas time when snow is thick on the ground. It's about Scrooge, a mean skinflint of an old lawyer who can't stand anyone enjoying Christmas. He refuses to give to charity, he refuses to go to his nephew's for Christmas lunch, he grudges giving his employee, Bob Cratchit, the day off for Christmas. 'Humbug!' he says to all these things, and he goes home to spend his Christmas alone in his gloomy old lodgings."

"Sounds just like my dad," said Zena, and everyone giggled.

"I shall tell him that when I next see him," said Mrs NcNab, wagging her finger playfully.

"So what happens to Scrooge?"

"He is haunted that night, first by the ghost of his old partner, now dead, Jacob Marley. And Jacob tells him that he is to be visited that Christmas by three terrifying ghosts, the Ghosts of Past, Present and Future. 'Humbug!' Scrooge says to this. But it happens. The Ghost of Christmas Past takes him back into his own past, and shows him what he was like then. He sees again his kind sister who rescued him from a dismal school. He sees again his old boss, Fezziwig, and his fellow apprentices in the warehouse where he got his first job. And lastly, he sees his fiancée, who rejected him because he put money before their happiness."

"That's weird, going back in the past," said Johnno. "Though, if you know anything about time-travel..."

"Not now, thank you, John," Mrs McNab butted in swiftly. She was well used to Johnno's rambling scientific theories, and this wasn't the time.

James was listening intently. There was

something about the idea of a ghost from the past that excited him, tied a knot in his stomach. "Go on," he said quietly, and Mrs McNab flashed him an understanding glance.

"The Ghost of Christmas Present is next, and he shows old Scrooge what Christmas is like at his clerk's – at Bob Cratchit's threadbare home. They are having a goose for Christmas lunch and everyone is happy to be together again, most of all his little lame son, Tiny Tim. Then Scrooge is whisked away to his nephew's where a party is going on. There he listens to everyone making fun of him... Scrooge realizes what a mean old misery he's been, but before he has a chance to reform, he gets an even worse fright. The Ghost of Christmas Future comes hard on the heels of the Past, and he is the most frightening of all. He is shrouded all in black and never speaks or shows his face. Just two luminous eyes glare at Scrooge in the dark..."

The class made exaggerated shivering, oohing and ahhing sounds.

"Shh," said Mrs McNab. "This is the really serious bit. Scrooge hears some businessmen he knows talking about someone's pitiful, lonely death. Then he is whisked to a dingy part of the town where a charwoman, a laundress and an undertaker are poring over old clothes, trinkets and bed-linen taken from someone's deathbed scene. And Scrooge gradually realizes that they're all talking about *his* death. Then he finds himself in his own bedroom, looking down at his own dead body..."

"That's horrible," Zena declared, pulling a face.

"It's meant to be," said Mrs McNab. "This is Charles Dickens, remember, not Walt Disney."

"Go on," James murmured.

"The Ghost takes him to Bob Cratchit's — where Tiny Tim is no more. Scrooge is so upset by this he knows for certain that he has to change his ways so that these things don't happen."

"How?" Johnno butted in, his brain

working furiously. "You can't change the future."

"Trust you to ask that, John," Mrs McNab sighed, though she was pleased he had none the less. "Dickens thought of that. There's a bit here... Ah, yes, listen to this. Dickens has Scrooge say, '*Men's courses will foreshadow certain ends, to which, if persevered in, they must lead. But if the courses be departed from, the ends will change.*' In other words, change your ways and you change your future. Now that's not a bad lesson for some of you, I should think! Anyway, that's what Scrooge did. He started by sending round a large turkey to the Cratchits' and then he spent Christmas day at his nephew's. He even gave his clerk, Bob Cratchit, a rise... He was transformed. There, that in a nutshell is the story of *A Christmas Carol*."

"So is that what we're going to act?" someone asked.

"Yes."

"Can I play one of the Cratchit girls?" Zena asked hopefully. Always get in first, was Zena's philosophy.

But it didn't work this time. "I'm not choosing parts yet. What I want you all to do is read the story over the half-term. Get to know it really well, inside out and back to front. That's your homework, OK? I've got some spare copies here, if anyone needs them."

After school, Zena and Johnno stood about in the playground with James. They pretended for a while to be the three ghosts.

The jolly Ghost of the Present appealed most to James, he seemed friendlier than the other two. But I don't want to be in the play, he thought. Joe would. Joe would love it. He'd be all three ghosts if he had the chance – and Marley's too.

He told Mum about *A Christmas Carol*. She fetched a copy of it from the bookcase. "This belonged to my mum," she said, running her hand over it fondly. "She had it when she was a girl. She read it to me, oh, several times, at Christmas." She looked at James uncertainly. "Would you like me to read it to you?"

James was surprised. She'd stopped reading to him ages ago. But he knew by the look on her face that, for some reason, this was different. "OK," he said with a casual nod.

And she began reading it to him that night.

Chapter 4

It was Saturday, the first day of half-term – the day before James came face to face with his brother's ghost. It was just an ordinary Saturday, he had no hint of what was going to happen – incredibly – the following day. Dad had cooked a rather chewy beef casserole for lunch. Mum was upstairs, a headache threatening. She got quite severe headaches from time to time. They made Dad tense and James feel helpless. That lunchtime she had bravely toyed with some of the beef but had left to go upstairs before the meal was over.

"Let's go for a walk," Dad suggested, putting the last of the crockery away.

"OK," said James, jumping at the chance to get out. "Where shall we go?"

"Doesn't matter. Anywhere. Get your trainers on."

They made their way down several streets to the river bank. Some swans and a gaggle of ducks swam towards them hopefully.

"We should have brought some bread," James said.

Dad didn't answer; he seemed rather silent.

They walked along the path above the river, Dad running his hand along the rail, James stopping to peer at the houseboats below.

They sat on a bench opposite a boat club and watched a boat crew lower their craft into the water. Once settled in, the rowers, at the command of their cox, moved with a single motion like a rowing machine, and swiftly cut through the dark water like a knife.

"You ought to try that one day," said Dad. "It's hard work but it can be fun."

James liked to sit beside the river, but

doing anything on it was something else. What if he capsized?

He heard Dad sigh. Was he thinking of Joe? It was a question James often asked himself. "I might do," he said, clearing his throat. "But I'll have to learn to swim first."

"Ah, swimming! I thought we gave up on that a long time ago," Dad said ironically.

"Things can change," James muttered.

Dad nodded, but his mind seemed to be on other things. "How do you like Mum reading to you again?" he said after a while.

James smiled. "I quite like it. It felt a bit odd at first, though."

"Oh? Why?"

James shrugged. "I don't know. Mum's voice sounded a bit funny. And then..."

James looked away. A boat chugged past them, swishing waves of water against the bank.

"And then?" Dad prompted.

"Well, it reminded me of when she used to read to both of us, Joe and me."

James felt Dad stiffen slightly.

"You said too much was left unsaid," he protested.

"No, it's not that. It's just that it would have reminded Mum too. You've probably noticed she's been a bit upset this weekend. She hasn't got over the birthday party yet."

"I know," James said.

They continued along the riverbank. When they reached the bridge, they climbed the steps to the road above and wandered back into the city. James became uneasy: they seemed to be heading for the block of flats where they had once lived. James had never been back there, although he had dreamt about them often enough, especially lately... On his walks with his parents they had always avoided going in that direction. When they were near to the *cul de sac* that led to the derelict flats, James tugged at Dad's sleeve. "Not that way, Dad," he said urgently.

"I heard it's about to be demolished at last," Dad said. "I just want to see it once more."

He saw the look of panic on his son's face.

"It won't do you any harm, James. You

have to face things, you know, everything, eventually. Otherwise you'll always be haunted by them."

"Like Mum?" James answered.

There was a flicker of surprise in Dad's eyes. He turned away. "You don't have to come if you don't want to. You could wait for me here."

Glancing quickly at his father's face, James said, "I'll come. It's only a building, after all." Dad gave a quick smile and they set off again.

They reached the rundown block of flats and peered through the wire mesh of the barriers.

"It was our first home together," Dad said. "We were very proud of it – even though it was a council place. And we liked the neighbours, they were a friendly lot. It may not look much now, but we enjoyed living there."

"And then Joe and me came along," James said, smiling.

Dad smiled too. "What a shock that was. Twins! We thought the place would be too small and we'd have to move, but somehow we managed. And there were always plenty of people to keep an eye on you."

"I liked living there too," James remembered. "Joe was always racing up and down the stairs and playing in the lift. It was fun."

"But eventually you got too big and noisy for the place." A sudden memory made him wince and he gripped the wire mesh. "It was the day after we signed the contract for the new house that Joe had his accident. Of course, the two events weren't connected, but it was merciful in a way. It kept your mother busy..."

An image came back to James of Mum just standing in front of the flats, defeated, refusing to come in. "She used to keep staring at that concrete bollard where we found Joe," he recalled.

"Well, I shall be glad when it's demolished. I feel sure that it will help Mum to know that it's no longer there. She's never been back here, you know, not since we moved." But even as he said that, he wondered whether it was true.

They wandered around the edge of the site. Everything looked dirty, abandoned, alone, except for a solitary almond tree that stood in the ragged grass, its leaves beginning to turn yellow. James recalled how the blossom used to blow about in the spring like pink snow, how Joe used to coax him up it, foothold by foothold, and hold on to him when he panicked at being so high.

"How many times did Joe fall from that tree?" Dad murmured. "And never once did he hurt himself. It's so ironic. He seemed to have bones like rubber."

They walked right round the block of flats and then started back up the street.

"There, that wasn't so bad, was it?" Dad said.

James shook his head. But he kept looking back at the lonely, receding building. A voice whispered in his head: *Come back. Don't go. Don't leave me here, not now you're so close*. He shivered. It reminded him of Joe's voice, the voice in his head, the way they used to talk to each other. Telepathy.

"Are you all right?" asked Dad.

James gave a brave smile and nodded.

"James," Dad said, clearing his throat.

James looked up at his father. By the change in the tone of his voice, he knew that his father was about to tell him something important, something that would cost him a good deal to say.

"I think you ought to know – you're old enough now – that it was only you that kept your mum and me together after Joe's death. I really believe that."

James walked on a few steps, replaying that extraordinary sentence in his head. Then he stopped. "What do you mean, Dad?"

"Your mother, she wasn't well, she blamed herself for Joe's death, and she took out all her anger on me. And I was angry with her too, but I tried not to show it, it wouldn't have been fair. I hope you didn't hear too many of those rows, we tried to shield you from them. If we hadn't had you to look after, I think we might have just split up."

James went very white. To have one's parents split up was every child's nightmare, and especially so for James.

Dad looked concerned. "I'm sorry, James. Perhaps I shouldn't have told you. It's just that I wanted you to know how important you were – you are – to both of us."

James was uneasy. Unusually for him, he took his father's hand and they walked on to the end of the street. "You *won't* split up, though, will you?" he suddenly said, urgently.

"Of course not," Dad said.

"But Mum isn't happy, is she?"

"No, not always. She still lives too much in the past. That's got to change."

"Is that why you wiped out Joe's name on the birthday cake?"

Dad smiled wryly. "Oh, you noticed that, did you? Well, Mum saw the sense in taking it off. I think she's trying now. That reading to you at night – that was her idea, you know. I'm so pleased she's doing it."

"Why?"

"Because she's doing it for you, not for a twin and his ghost, but just for you."

That cheered James a little.

He thought about his mother sitting by his

bed softly reading *A Christmas Carol*. It took him back to a time when he and Joe used to snuggle up in the bottom bunk bed together, listening to her voice as it lulled them to sleep.

Mum's headache eased off that evening, but she did not quite feel up to reading to James another instalment of *A Christmas Carol* that night. As his parents usually slept in on a Sunday, he was allowed to stay up late watching a video with Dad.

He slipped quickly into sleep and had one of those nights that seemed full of active dreams, bright, confusing and strange. When he woke from nights like this, he often felt that on the other side of sleep he lived another, totally different life. Which was the real one?

Towards morning, when he was half-awake, he dreamt he was walking down the *cul de sac* towards the flats. Blossom swirled all about him, settling on roofs and gardens and cars, glittering in his hair. As he reached the flats, the last petal was torn from the tree and swirled away, so that the night was suddenly clear. He looked back and saw the flakes melting on the ground like snow. His own footprints burnt electric blue on the ground.

In the dark building their window on the fifth floor glowed mysteriously. He picked up a stone from the road. It was heavy and cold and he had great difficulty in raising it, in hurling it at the glowing window. The glass did not shatter, it dissolved on impact. And then there was Joe, a barely visible, ghostly Joe, perched on the windowsill. He jumped. James wanted to scream a warning, but Joe floated down on a parachute and tumbled over, laughing.

Silently, they followed the trail of blue electric footprints down the street. With each step Joe took, he seemed to become more visible, more solid. James could hardly keep up with him. Why didn't Joe say anything? Or look at him?

When they arrived home, James drifted in, as if he too was a ghost, but Joe could go no further. Now James was at the window and

Joe outside, but this time there was no stone to throw.

James woke, struggled out of bed and pulled back the curtains. The road was empty. He stared unseeing: was there a message in that dream? A message from Joe?

He had to go back to the flat. Perhaps Joe was there. What he meant by "there" he did not attempt to define: it was more a feeling.

Later, he watched Mum settle down in the conservatory, switch on the radio and close her eyes. He stood in the hall and listened to the click of Dad's fingers on the computer in the study. Each had withdrawn into their own lives, as they often did on Sunday afternoons. It was the perfect time for James to slip away.

Going out to play. Back for tea, he scribbled on a piece of paper. His hand shook as he quietly closed the front door. It would have shaken even more if he'd known that within an hour his brother's ghost would be materializing before his very eyes.

* * * *

James carried the pale ball of light that was Joe's ghost all the way home through the quiet streets, balancing it like a precious egg in his hands. He felt so elated, he was not aware of anything else: the people who peered from their windows, the curious passers-by, or the woman who crossed herself in her little front garden.

By the time he reached his street late that afternoon his fingers and palms were numb with cold and his arms were shivering. But he didn't care, he was too wildly excited. He had found his brother again. He was bringing Joe home.

Just *how* much his life had changed that afternoon, he would discover in the strange, uncanny days that lay ahead.

He reached the front door.

Calm down, James, said Joe. *You don't want Mum and Dad getting suspicious. They could spoil it all.*

James hadn't thought of that. *I can't tell them?*

Of course not. They wouldn't believe you. They'd think you've gone mad.

But you could tell them. You could appear to them like you did to me.

I'm a ghost, James, remember?

Then why did you appear to me?

Because I need you. You need me. We're two halves of the same being. I've learnt that, at least, on the other side.

But...

There's no use in arguing about this, James. It's just you and me, OK?

James nodded. He knew that Joe was right, although he couldn't say why. Besides, in the past he'd been used to doing as Joe told him: it was comforting to fall back into that old pattern again.

I'm going to make myself invisible now, James. It'd be a bit hard to explain to Mum and Dad how you came to be carrying a little ball of light, wouldn't it?

James smiled. He watched the ball of light fade into nothing.

Joe, are you still there?

Right by your side.

James was greeted at the front door by Mum waving his note. "This isn't good enough, James. Where have you been?"

He wiped his feet slowly, thinking, what shall I tell her?

Tell her the truth.

"I've been back to the flats, Mum," he blurted out. "They're going to knock them down."

Mum blanched. He could see she was about to say something hurtful, then she bit it back.

"I had to, Mum," he pleaded. "I dreamt about the place and, and about ... Joe. I had to go back one more time."

Mum's face softened and she put an arm around his shoulder. He could feel her trembling slightly. "I know, James, don't worry. Your father's been on at me today to do the same. What good he thinks it will do, I don't know, especially as he is the one who's always complaining that we live in the past."

Tell her it doesn't matter now.

"It doesn't matter now, Mum. It's only an empty shell."

She looked at him searchingly. "Are you sorry you went?"

"Oh, no," he said, with a sudden smile. "But I shan't be going back there again."

He was wrong there. He would go back to it one more time, and for the same reason, and in desperation, but that had yet to be faced.

He made to go upstairs to his room, conscious of Joe, like a guilty secret, hovering unseen beside him.

"There's something I want to talk to you about," Mum said, "before you go upstairs."

"I'll be down in a minute," he said urgently.

Once in the bedroom, Joe materialized. He was grinning and shaking, almost dancing in the air. *This is amazing, James, amazing. I'm home!*

James could only laugh too.

Go down to Mum, said Joe. *I need time to get used to this.*

But James was too excited to go down immediately. He went into the bathroom and stared at his flushed face in the mirror. *I've got Joe*, he said to himself. *I've got him back.* But he felt immediately that wasn't quite right. *His ghost then, the bit of him that lives on for ever. And he can look just like he would have done if he had lived. I couldn't hope for any more.*

He drew a deep breath. How on earth was he going to keep it from Mum?

Slowly, his heart still thumping wildly, he went downstairs.

She was sitting in the kitchen sipping a mug of tea. He fetched from the fridge a bottle of lemonade and took great gulps.

"Put it in a glass, James. I've told you about that before."

Obediently, he did as he was told. Each minute of this ordinariness helped to calm him down.

"Have you been running? You look a bit flushed."

He shook his head and sat down opposite her.

"Now listen, James. I've had an idea. Or your teacher has."

James tried very hard to focus on what she was saying. "Mrs McNab?"

"Yes, who else? She rang me. We haven't spoken for ages. I was quite pleased to hear from her."

"What did she say about me?" James asked nervously.

"She thinks it would be a good idea if you took part in the Christmas drama production."

"Oh?" James was surprised. Drama was hardly his best subject.

"Yes, and I do too. It will help to bring you out of yourself, give you some confidence."

It's likely to do just the opposite, James thought gloomily. He'd love to act in the play, to be a star and gain the class's admiration, but he was too quiet, too shy, too stammery: it was impossible.

She saw the look on his face. "Please, James, think about it. I think it would be the best thing for you."

"I can't."

"Just give it a try, eh?"

James was about to give a decisive shake of his head when he was interrupted. *Don't disappoint her, James. Say yes.*

Joe? Are you in this room? He looked around wildly.

No, I'm still upstairs, but I can see through walls, you know, just like any other ghost. James could even hear Joe chuckle.

"James," said Mum. "What's the matter?"

"Oh, nothing," he mumbled.

Look, with me beside you, and giving you energy, telling you what to do and say, this play will be a piece of cake. Go on, say you'll do it.

You mean it?

Of course.

"OK, Mum, if Mrs McNab thinks I can do it, then I'll have a go. But don't blame me if I make a mess of it." He giggled nervously, the pressure of his feelings very near the surface now.

Mum smiled and patted his hand on the table. "That's great. But you mustn't get all worked up about it. I'll help you with your words and the costume. You'll be all right, you'll see."

James, in his pyjamas, looked searchingly around his bedroom.

Where are you? Are you invisible again?

No. I'm a ball of light this time. I'm counting to a hundred. You've got that long to find me.

James smiled. They'd often played hide-and-seek in the past. He began to pull open drawers, look behind curtains and under the bed, search in his wardrobe.

Thirty-seven, thirty-eight, thirty-nine...

I can't find you. Where are you?

"James, what are you looking for?" Mum was standing just inside the door, holding *A Christmas Carol*.

"Oh, nothing," he said, confused.

Mum eyed him suspiciously; she always knew when her son wasn't telling the truth. But she decided not to press him. "Do you want the next chapter? We're about to meet the Ghost of Christmas Past."

"Yes, please," said James eagerly, jumping into bed.

Mum sat in the chair beside him and reminded him about the ghost of Jacob Marley who had come to Scrooge on Christmas Eve and promised three hauntings. As she began to read, James looked up at the light hanging from the ceiling, the light bulb shielded by a white paper sphere. Didn't it seem much brighter than usual?

Mum began reading. " *'The curtains of the bed were drawn aside, I tell you, by a hand. Not the curtains at his feet, nor the curtains at his back, but those to which his face was addressed. The curtains of his bed were drawn aside; and Scrooge, starting up into a half-recumbent attitude, found himself face to face with the unearthly visitor who drew them...'* "

Mum paused. "Perhaps I shouldn't be reading this just before going to sleep. It might give you nightmares."

"Of course not, Mum."

No, do go on. This sounds good.

James glanced up at the light and smiled. Joe was listening too.

" *'It was a strange figure – like a child: yet not so like a child as an old man... Its hair, which hung about its neck and down its back, was white as if with age; and yet the face had not a wrinkle in it...'* "

James listened to the strangest description

of a ghost he'd ever heard. Joe, in comparison, was simplicity itself.

I could look like that if I wanted to, said Joe.

Really? Can you change your appearance that much?

Yeah, I think so, so long as I've got enough energy.

You mean energy from other people?

Yes. Like when we exchanged energy in the flat. That blue current...

"James, are you listening to this?"

"Of course, Mum."

" '...*its belt sparkled and glittered now in one part, now in another, and what was light one instant, at another time was dark, so the figure itself fluctuated ... being now a figure with one arm, now with one leg, now with twenty legs...*' "

"Twenty legs?" James exclaimed, wriggling his own legs about in amusement.

Piece of cake to us ghosts.

" '...*now a pair of legs without a head, now a head without a body...*

" ' "*Are you the Spirit, sir, whose coming was foretold to me?*" asked Scrooge.

" ' "*I am!*"

" 'The voice was soft and gentle. Singularly low, as if instead of being so close beside him, it was at a distance.

" ' "Who, and what are you?" Scrooge demanded.

" ' "I am the Ghost of Christmas Past." ' "

Joe closed his eyes. The language of the story was often hard and strange, but the way Mum read it, he had no difficulty in seeing the story unfold in his mind. What a strange story too. Scrooge drifted back like a ghost himself and saw so many people he used to know, as if the Past hadn't disappeared for ever but still existed, like a film you could play over again and again. *Is it really like that, Joe?*

I don't know. I'm stuck in the Present, remember?

Chapter 5

For the first couple of days of half-term James was happy to stay indoors, keeping mainly to his room: he had Joe to talk to. They had so much catching up to do. Joe questioned James about all that had happened since his death; his curiosity seemed endless. All James had to do was lie on his bed and listen to the two voices in his head, his own and Joe's. When Mum came in to see what he was doing, he always pretended to be reading *A Christmas Carol* or to be looking at the bird-identification CD-Rom on his computer. Of course, it did get a bit tiring at times, for Joe would never let up. Perhaps he was making up for all the years of being a silent ghost.

Mum was pleased that he was taking so much interest in the book, and Dad was hopeful that the CD-Rom would at last teach his son something about ornithology, but by the third day they became a little uneasy. James seemed preoccupied, wrapped up in a secret of his own. They talked about it together after he had gone to bed: was it something they should worry about, or should they leave well alone?

"Perhaps it's the thought of being in the school play," said Mum. "Perhaps he's wanted to do something like that for ages but lacked the confidence."

"Yes, it's all to do with confidence, isn't it? He's never had much of that. Maybe he's growing up at last."

"I'm not sure that's fair."

"Well, you know what I mean. I tell you one thing, I don't think it's healthy for him to hang around the house all day. He should be out with his friends. I really think it's about time you let go a bit, Janice. Began to trust him."

She knew he was right. "What do you

suggest, then? We could go out visiting, or..."

"No, he's got to start making his own way without us. I mean, when I was his age I was always out of the house, fishing all day by the river with my mates or going to see a film."

Mum sighed. "OK," she said, a little stiffly, for she was being criticized here. "I'll talk to him about it tomorrow."

Upstairs, in James's room, Joe had materialized. James, sitting on the bed, hugged his knees, still in a daze at having his almost-solid-looking brother there beside him again. It stirred up such a strange mixture of emotions: excitement, grief, gratitude, wonder.

They're talking about you.

What are they saying?

They say you should get out more.

Mum doesn't like me going out.

Well, Dad's said you should. He says you lack confidence.

Really?

Yeah, but now that we're together again, that'll be a thing of the past.

You think so? How come?

I can only live in the real world through you, right? So we'll become like one person. I was never afraid of anything, remember? I'll be there whenever you get scared. Just like I used to be.

Thanks, Joe.

James hugged himself tighter. He had almost forgotten what it was like to be happy: now, suddenly, the world had changed.

"Why don't you ring that friend of yours, what's his name? The one that's always talking about planets and space and things."

"Johnno?"

He hesitated by the phone. He could see Mum was making a real effort to behave differently and it made him nervous.

"I don't know his number."

Oh, come on, James. Look it up. Don't play into her hands.

James pulled out the telephone directory and together he and Mum found the number. But when he dialled it, there was no answer.

He thought Mum looked slightly relieved, but she said, "What about Zena?"

He wasn't sure he wanted to spend the day with Zena. She was all right at school, but he'd never met her outside school. She'd be really surprised if he rang her.

"I've heard a lot about this Zena from Mrs McNab. She's sounds fun. Come on, James, find her number."

Zena lived only a few streets away. She had many brothers and sisters, all much older than her – she was the "baby" of the family – but she often felt left out of things, especially during the holidays when the family were all at work or college. So she was delighted when James rang and asked, hesitantly, if she was doing anything that morning.

Mum gave him enough money to buy lunch out, and then she tucked an extra ten pound note into his pocket. "Treat yourself," she said. She put a comb through his hair, studying his face as she did so. "There's something going on in that head of yours," she said with a smile. "Which I don't understand. But whatever it is, it's doing you good. Now, have you decided what you're going to do?"

He shook his head.

Tell her you're going swimming.

But I don't want to.

You do! You were telling me the other night that you wished you could conquer your fear of water, remember. You said you were the only one in your class who couldn't swim and that made you feel an idiot. I learnt to swim like a fish before I died. I'll be there to teach you.

"I think we might go to the leisure pool," he said quietly to Mum.

She looked surprised, then a little anxious. "Zena can swim, I take it?"

"She's got certificates for it."

"Well, promise me you'll keep out of the deep pool. Stick to the learners' pool, OK?"

"Of course, Mum."

"Have you got your swimming gear?"

He went upstairs to fetch it.

I'm coming too, said Joe.

But I can't carry you like I did before. Zena would freak out!

I'll have to make myself invisible.

Have you got enough energy for that?

We'll see.

You could take some of mine.

Better not, James. You'll be the one who gets tired then.

James watched Joe fade into nothingness. It gave him a sharp stab of panic, as if he was losing his brother again. He reached out; the air where Joe had been was very cold.

Don't worry, I'm still here.

But how will I know if you're there?

You'll know. The air is always icy where I am.

Mum watched James from the front door as he swung his bag down the street. There was a little lump in her throat, and when she closed the door the house felt very empty. But for once she did not mind.

As soon as he appeared, Zena burst out of her house, slamming the door behind her, then raced back to get her swimming gear. She seemed more than usually boisterous, but as they walked down towards the Common, she gradually calmed down.

"I was stuck in there with Rita, you know, my second big sister? She keeps on at me to do this, be that; she never lets up."

She looked at him shyly, still trying to work out why, after all this time, he should suddenly ask her out. But as usual, he was staring straight ahead, or looking at his feet, in a world of his own. She'd spent the weekend with her cousins in Croydon and now, to fill the silence, she set about describing each one, mercilessly picking on their weaknesses and making them sound so funny James was soon laughing.

Phew! She doesn't stop, does she? said Joe. James looked up. *Yes, I'm still here. I can see why you like her. Not a dull moment with her around!*

They came to the children's playground. Zena looked absurdly large on the swing but she didn't care. She went higher and higher, whooping and shouting, "I'm on a trapeze." She almost went full-circle, but in the end, didn't dare: one day she would, she promised herself.

"I'm dizzy," she said, landing uncertainly

on the ground. James laughed as she wandered around, pretending to have lost all sense of direction. "My head is spinning."

"It'll spin off into space," he giggled.

Abruptly, she turned to him. "Now it's your turn. Go on, I'll give you a push."

"No way," he said, jumping up from the swing where he'd been gently swaying back and forth. The truth was, he'd never learnt to do it: fear of heights had always got the better of him.

"You can't do it," Zena mocked, pointing a finger.

"I can. I just don't feel like it."

"Prove it, then."

He shook his head.

What are you afraid of, James? I can do it, you know that.

Yes, but I can't.

Do you want to do it?

Of course I do. I always have.

Then let me help you.

How?

Touch me.

I thought you said we weren't to touch.

Yes, but the energy can flow both ways. I can give you some of my energy – and my confidence. And then you'll be able – we'll be able – to fly up on that swing.

"James," said Zena, suddenly still. "Your eyes have gone funny. Are you all right?"

James rubbed his eyes and then looked at the swing. "Will you give me a push?" he said to Zena.

She grinned and positioned herself behind the swing.

"Now, close your eyes," said James.

"What for?"

"Never you mind."

"You're not going to run off, are you?"

James winced at that. "Of course not," he said. "But if you want me to go on the swing, you've got to close your eyes and count to a hundred."

Somewhat intrigued, Zena did as she was told. Of course, she peered through her long eyelashes to see what he was up to. He was reaching out with his hand, as if looking for something in the air... What was that? A flash of blue, crackly light? It couldn't be! But something had happened, for his eyes were closed and his body was trembling slightly. Whatever was he up to?

"I'm ready," he said, springing up.

She thought, *he's different*. His eyes, his face, the way he moves... But he was already sitting on the swing. She gave him a hefty push and stood back. She could see at once that he knew what to do. He flew back and forth in ever-widening arcs, swifter and swifter, until he was describing half a circle.

This is fantastic. The voice could have been his own or Joe's, he couldn't tell.

Higher. Higher.

The world swung high before his eyes and he suddenly felt like a bird swooping into the sky.

Go on, right over. Just once. That was clearly Joe's voice.

Have you ever done it?

Once. It was the scariest thing I'd ever done. But I was only seven then.

Mum would have died if she'd known.

Well, she didn't know. Let's do it. Let's go right over.

I daren't. I shall come off.

You won't. Come on. Just this once.

No.

Do it for me, then.

James felt a powerful new surge of energy in his legs. He pushed harder and harder at each swing, his heart in his mouth.

Below, Zena watched anxiously, sensing something quite out of the ordinary was happening before her eyes.

Suddenly, he flew right over on the tail-end of a gigantic push, tracing a giant circle in the air. The world swung upside down. It was exhilarating – and terrifying. As soon as he was heading back down towards earth, he knew he could not do it again, Joe or no Joe, and with all his might he applied the body's brakes.

Once back on firm ground, he felt sick. He lay on the grass, his chest heaving, the sky swimming crazily above him.

"That was amazing, James," Zena said, kneeling beside him. "Amazing."

"Terrifying," said James; but he was grinning. And he could hear Joe laughing inside his head.

They swung their bags back and forth as they made their way across the Common.

"They'll never believe me," Zena was saying. "When I tell them at school what you just did. You'll have to do it again, to show them. It was incredible. I've never been able to get up that high. You'll have to show me how to do it. I mean, *how did you do it?*"

James wasn't listening. He stopped. His face was suddenly full of fear.

"What's the matter?" Zena was alarmed. Then she saw the large herd of cows munching hay near the exit. They would have to pass through that herd to get to the road. Even Zena felt a little nervous of them.

Ignore them, James. They're quite stupid and harmless.

James tightened his grip on his bag's shoulder strap. *You don't remember, do you?*

It all flashed again before him.

He and Joe were out walking in the woods with their dog Sheba. Mum and Dad had fallen behind. The boys came out into a field where there was a herd of cattle. Sheba ran among them, barking and snapping at them. Joe rushed in after her, jumping and shouting and chasing the dog, thoroughly disturbing the cattle, among which were young calves. When James shouted to Joe to come back, Sheba raced towards him. And then, as if with one mind, the herd turned on the dog and thundered after it. Suddenly, huge, lumbering animals were snorting and thudding directly towards James. He'd never felt so terrified in his life. Joe shot past him, grabbing him as he ran, and they hurtled back towards the wood with the cows snorting hot, furious breath at their heels. Just in time, they made the safety of the wood. James collapsed, white and tearful, and had to be carried home.

Zena watched his eyes. They seemed to flicker inward, like the eyes of a blind person, and then outward again: it was very strange.

"They give me the creeps, too," she said, regarding the cows critically.

James was in a sweat. "Let's go round to the other way out," he mumbled.

A teasing look came into Zena's eyes. "You're not afraid?" she began.

"You're scared too," James accused her.

She'll never let you live it down, Bruv. She'll tell everyone at school. You've got to get through them. Touch me again. Together, it'll be easy.

"I'm not," Zena protested. "They don't scare me, not really."

But both could see that the cattle did scare her. The difference was, Zena had the courage to face them. She began to move forward, into the herd, stepping warily, keeping her eyes straight ahead. The cows went on munching, barely glancing at her.

James was trembling. It seemed only yesterday to him that that herd of cattle was thundering after him, about to trample him into the ground.

Touch me, James.

James did not hesistate any longer. He reached out and touched the cold invisibility that was Joe. In a few seconds a current of energy shot up through his arm and into his body. His fear dissolved.

Zena glanced back and saw him hurrying towards her, grinning as if it had all been a joke.

They ran the last few metres through the cattle to the gate, laughing with relief as soon as they made the pavement on the other side.

"That was really silly," said Zena. "Fancy being scared of those stupid old things."

"I wasn't," said James half-truthfully.

James shut the door of the cubicle in the leisure pool changing area.

Are you still with me, Joe?

Of course. I'll be right by you all the time. If you get really scared, just touch me, OK?

James hugged the towel to his chest. This was proving to be one of the most extraordinary mornings of his life. He was no longer alone. He had his twin brother with him at every step. Happiness filled him. He stepped out of the changing-room with a confidence he had never felt before.

Zena was already in the deep pool. She was

a good swimmer, moving swiftly through the water with the minimum of effort, her head bobbing up and down in waves of reflected light. She paused to watch James step across to the shallow pool. Although he was small and slender for his age, he seemed to walk taller than she'd known before, almost eager to get to the water. He is *different* today, she thought, watching him with fascination. Whatever has happened to him?

James splashed about in the learner pool for a while, but he felt out of place there. It was full of mothers with babies and pre-schoolers. *Yeah, that's baby stuff*, said Joe from somewhere above his head, his patience soon running out.

But I'm not ready for the big pool yet.

Well, go in the whirlpool, then. I always used to like that.

Zena joined him there, and they splashed about among the bubbles, driving everyone else away.

They got some canned drinks from a vending machine and stood by a huge, straggling pot-plant, watching kids swishing down the chute and rolling into the water below.

"I'm going on that next," Zena said. "It's the best thing here. Are you coming on it?"

James shook his head. "You know I can't swim," he said quietly.

"Oh, yeah, I forgot. It's funny, that, you not being able to swim."

"I wish I could."

"What's stopping you, then?"

"Dunno."

Zena felt sorry for him. She couldn't imagine what it was like to be afraid of the water.

"You could go on the chute, though," she said. "It lands in quite shallow water. You can stand up in it."

"I don't like putting my head under water."

"You could wear my goggles. That'll protect your eyes. And I'll be at the bottom to catch you when you come down."

She's right, James.

I'll do it if you let me touch you.

OK. But not for too long. I'm beginning to feel a bit tired.

"Give us your goggles, then," he said to Zena, pretending, by the tone of his voice, that he was only doing this because she was being tiresomely insistent.

Zena giggled. She put the goggles on him herself.

As they walked over to the steps leading to the chute, James paused and groped in the air around him. Once more, he felt Joe's cold energy flow into him. His fear of the water faded away at once.

But for a few brief, ugly moments, a little shadow was cast over that morning's triumphs. Standing in the queue waiting to mount the chute steps were two boys from James's school. They weren't exactly bullies, but they liked to push their weight around and they were expert at cruel teasing. James had more than once been their victim.

Zena hadn't noticed them, or if she had she was ignoring them. She saw a girl she knew further up the queue and, shouting a greeting, she went up to talk to her. The boys thought this was queue-jumping and they protested. She told them to leave her alone, but that only provoked them further. With ugly expressions on their faces, they started pushing her away from her friend, back towards the end of the queue.

Don't just stand there, James. Do something.

James, with Joe's confidence coursing through him, strode up to the boys. "You leave her alone," he shouted, pushing one of them away from Zena.

They looked at him in astonishment.

"What's it to you, Hurrell?" one of the boys demanded.

"She's my friend. We're together. Now, leave off."

"Your *friend*, eh?" the other boy sneered.

"Your *black* friend," said the first, loading the word with as much contempt as he could express.

James saw red. He seized the boy's hand and with surprising force he twisted it up behind the boy's back. The boy gasped from pain and bent forward. The other boy was about to go to his rescue.

"I shouldn't, if I were you," said James, and he jerked the boy's arm up harder, making him howl.

Suddenly ashamed, the boy gritted his teeth and muttered, "Sorry."

"Now you," said Zena, turning to the other boy. But he backed away, and when he was far enough he shouted, "Get lost."

James let go of the boy he was holding and pushed him away in disgust.

"Get out of here," he threatened.

The two boys slunk away, shouting unconvincing threats. The queue clapped and cheered.

Zena did not know what to say. She was shaken by the experience. She was about to fling her arms around James and give him a kiss of thanks, but even as she stepped forward to do so she saw that the expression in his eyes had turned inward again, and she stopped.

We acted as one there, James. By instinct. Didn't it make you feel good?

Yeah. But that's not how I behave at all.

No, but it's how we behave. You know, this doing things together, as one, is better than when

I was alive, when we were two. Just think about it, James. We're going to have some real fun together.

James stretched his arms up in the air and laughed.

The attendant, who had witnessed the end of this little fracas, and had been about to intervene, now called James and Zena to the foot of the chute stairs. "I think they deserve to jump the queue, don't you?" he said to the line of people.

Zena took James's hand and they climbed the stairs together.

"I'll go first, OK, and I'll be there to catch you when you come down."

They stood together at the top of the chute. Water funnelled down the slides. The foaming pool below seemed very far away.

Are you still with me, Joe?

Would you have got this far if I wasn't?

Zena launched herself down the chute, squealing with delight.

Then, casting his fear aside, James sat at the top of the chute and felt the tug of the water. He loosened his grip...

Here we go, Joe, he shouted inside his head.

Then he was hurtling down. Neither he nor his brother had ever felt anything so exhilarating as that seemingly endless descent down the chute and the splash in the water below.

James sat up in bed, waiting for Mum to come in to read the next part of *A Christmas Carol*.

You're very quiet, Joe.

I'm tired. You drained off quite a lot of energy from me today.

But it was great, though, wasn't it? One of the best days of my life!

Yeah, it was kinda weird.

Joe?

Yeah?

Are you sure you're all right?

'Course.

I get the feeling you aren't.

Oh, well...

Yes?

It's just that... Well, it's a bit frustrating, you know, being a ghost. I can only really watch from the sidelines.

I thought you and I did everything together. I thought what I did, you did. Isn't that what you said?

Yes. But it's not the same as being alive, is it?

No, I suppose not.

James was silent for a while, thinking about this. He began to feel sorry for his ghostly twin.

"Now then, where did we get to?" Mum murmured as she turned the pages of the book.

"We're about to meet the second ghost," James said eagerly.

"Ah, yes." She began to read.

Are you listening to this Joe?

Every word. Now, sh!

" ' "*Come in!*" *exclaimed the Ghost.* "*Come in! and know me better, man!*"

" '*Scrooge entered timidly, and hung his head before this Spirit...*

" ' "*I am the Ghost of Christmas Present,*" *said the Spirit.* "*Look upon me!*"

" '*Scrooge reverently did so. It was clothed in one simple green robe, or mantle, bordered with white fur...*

" ' "You've never liked me before!" exclaimed the Spirit.

" ' "Never," Scrooge made to answer...' "

James snuggled down in his bed and listened to the tale of the Cratchits' poor but happy Christmas lunch of goose and Christmas pudding. For a while he forgot all about Joe.

Joe, however, didn't always listen to the story. He'd learnt something today, he'd learnt what it really meant to be a ghost in a world of flesh and blood: he could do things through his brother, but not on his own. It had been fun, but vague doubts began to nag at him. He looked down on the tranquil scene: his mother reading softly, his brother's head just poking above the sheet. How he wished he could be alive again!

Chapter 6

After James had fallen asleep, Joe hovered about the room for a while, feeling restless. Then he floated downstairs, pausing to look in on his parents in the living-room. They were watching the television in the dark. Strange emotions flickered through him, like blue light on shimmering cloth. What did he feel for them now? A longing to be with them again, and an emptiness. But they were worlds apart: there was no crossing that gulf.

His mother turned her head and looked at the door.

Joe moved away. One thing he was sure of: after years of loneliness, drifting through distortions of time, or haunting the flat, he had come home again.

On the landing wall there was a large mirror. Doesn't superstition say that ghosts have no reflection? If that was so, he thought, perhaps I am no longer quite a ghost. With an effort of will, he slowly materialized. Now he was looking at himself as a boy, the spitting image of James except for the moonlit pallor of his skin and the strange opaque look in his eyes.

Someone came out of the living-room downstairs.

Before he had time to dissolve, he looked down the stairs – straight into the eyes of his mother.

She gasped and clutched the bannister to steady herself. In horror, she watched as the boy – was it Joe? – dissolved into mist.

"Donald," she cried weakly. " Come out here."

Her heart was thumping wildly.

"What is it? Are you all right?"

She pointed to the landing with a trembling finger. "I saw... Oh, Donald, I think I saw Joe, up there, like a ghost." She covered her face and moaned.

Dad put his arms around her. "Don't be silly, love. It must have been James."

"No," she said, shaking her head fiercely.

He watched her helplessly. "Look, let's go up and see."

They climbed the stairs to James's room.

Dad looked down at his sleeping son, and then at his wife's stricken face. He felt uneasy. He looked around the room as if he might see something hovering in the shadows.

The next morning, James met Zena and Johnno on the Common. Although it was late October, it wasn't too cold, the sun shone and there was a bright, brittle light.

Zena kicked the first of the fallen leaves into the air and then picked up a long twig. "I am the Ghost of Christmas Present," she laughed, waving the twig about; she too had been reading the story.

They walked along the riverbank path, then sat on a bench. Zena fished from her bag a lump of bread, and soon there was a noisy riot of swans, ducks and geese squabbling over it.

Johnno stared at the misty disc of moon still hanging in the sky. "Why is it," he said, "that the moon is still up there in broad daylight? It looks like the ghost of a planet, doesn't it?"

"Oh, you believe in ghosts, then?" James asked.

"Don't know. Is there any proof for them?"

"I believe in them," Zena declared, throwing the last of the bread to the birds.

"But have you ever met one?" Johnno challenged her.

"No way," she answered, shivering dramatically.

"I certainly don't believe in the Dickens kind of ghost," said Johnno contemptuously. "Straight out of his imagination."

"But you're going to be in the play, though?" said Zena.

Johnno shook his head.

"Oh, go on. I saw you as Mr Fezziwig."

"Mr who?"

"He was Scrooge's first boss. He gave a wonderful party on Christmas Eve for all his poor apprentices."

Johnno shrugged. He turned to James. "What about you, James? Are you going to be in this play?"

"Yeah," James smiled. "I'm going to play the ghost."

"Which one?"

"Dunno." Then he grinned. "All three of them, perhaps!"

"See," said Zena, digging Johnno in the ribs. "I told you he was different. Something's happened to him this holiday."

James laughed. Johnno looked at him through his horn-rimmed spectacles with renewed interest.

"What shall we do, then?" Zena asked. "Any ideas?"

James had been watching a punt float down river under a bridge. "I know," he exclaimed, fishing in his pocket. "Let's hire a punt." He drew out the ten pound note Mum had given him the day before. Zena was noisy in her approval of this idea; Johnno nodded and said, "Why not?"

They hurried towards the bridge where the punts were for hire.

You're very quiet today, James said to Joe.

I'm tired. You didn't half take it out of me yesterday.

Sorry. Are you all right, though?

Yeah, fine. I shall enjoy myself through you, today.

There was only one punt available, poled by a scruffy youth in an anorak. He did not seem very pleased to see them. "Last week of the season," he said as they climbed into the punt. "If you'd turned up two days from now, you'd have been out of luck," he added with evident satisfaction. "Now, I don't want any trouble. Keep still at all times, don't move about the punt. I don't want us capsizing."

"But I can't swim," James said, staring at the muddy water.

"Well, don't expect me to fish you out," said the youth, grimly.

Zena managed to keep still for the first five minutes, but soon she was swivelling around in her scat, jumping up and down, pointing and exclaiming at everything she saw.

"Can't you keep still?" the punter ordered, giving her a dirty look.

They drifted on in an uncomfortable silence. The buildings of the city soon gave way to fields and trees. Zena trailed her hand in the water and pulled faces at Johnno.

As he pushed at his pole and panted at the effort, the punter seemed to be getting more and more bad-tempered. Each time a motorboat chugged past, creating a backwash which rocked the punt, he swore loudly at them.

About a mile or so out of the city, they came to a landing-stage.

"Here's where we turn back," the punter said, wiping his brow.

Zena glanced swiftly at the other two. She did not relish the thought of another hour in the punt with him. "Why don't we get out and walk back?" she said eagerly to the others, and before they could consider it, she was already clambering out.

"Here, what're you doing?" the punter protested.

"We're getting out here," said Johnno. "We've had enough of you."

"Yeah," said James, following quickly.

"Suit yourselves," said the punter.

They watched him punt swiftly back down the water until he disappeared out of sight around a bend.

"Good riddance, you stupid git!" Zena shouted, releasing some of the tension that had built up inside each of them. Hysterically, they fell about laughing.

Then they sat on the landing-stage, trailing long dry stalks in the water, waving to the motorboats, listening to the plop of the fish when all was quiet.

Johnno looked at his watch. "We'll have to get moving," he said. "It'll be lunchtime before we get back."

They skirted fields and climbed through wire fences, forever wondering guiltily if they were trespassing. They came up against a wide ditch half-full with greenish, weed-choked water. It was too wide to jump.

"We can't go back," Zena wailed.

"We could go round it," said James; but they found it stretched to the horizon, and cows were grazing up ahead.

"All we need is a log to put across it," said Johnno.

They found a fallen tree in a copse nearby. It was about the right size but it took ages to break off the small branches and twigs to make it fairly smooth. They dragged it to the ditch and then had further difficulty in lodging it securely on the other side. By the time they had done it, they were feeling hot and dirty.

"I'll go first," said Zena. Spreading her arms, she walked along the narrow, bending log with barely a wobble or a hesitation. "Easy," she shouted from the other side.

Johnno went next. Being bigger and less agile, he was much less confident. In the middle of the log, he slipped. Luckily, his legs slid either side of the log, and he just managed to hold on to it. He half-slid along on his bottom for the remainder of the crossing, scratching himself on the jagged remains of the twigs and shouting, "Ow!" every two seconds. Zena pulled him on to the bank the other side.

Johnno's slip and cries had unnerved James. He put his foot on the log, then panicked.

"I can't," he shouted.

"Go on, James. It's much easier than you think," Zena shouted encouragingly.

James swallowed hard, clutched his bag tightly, and put his foot back on. But it was no good.

"Sit on it like I did," Johnno suggested, "and shuffle along."

He did that and it got him almost half way across. But by then he was sweating with a fear he could not understand. He was too terrified to go forward, too terrified to go back.

Help me, Joe.

There's nothing to be afraid of.

Just help me.

OK. Now, hold the log tightly with your right

hand. Got it? Now reach out to your left. I'm right beside you.

James felt the cold energy flow up his arm and into his body. He leapt up on the log, suddenly brimming with confidence.

"Just kidding you," he shouted with a laugh, and he sailed nonchalantly along the rest of the log, hardly looking at where he was placing his feet.

"You could have fooled me," said Johnno, staring at him wide-eyed.

"He's a good actor," said Zena, patting him on the back. But then she stiffened, her eyes went wide. Her hand fell away from his back and pointed waveringly above the ditch. "What is that?" she whispered, fear catching her breath.

James turned. "Joe!" he shouted.

Johnno stared in disbelief, his glasses glinting in the pale light.

Joe had materialized, a ball of light above the log.

I'm sorry, James. I can't stay invisible any more today. I've used up too much energy. I've got to go.

111

No. Joe, don't leave me.

Joe said no more. He sped away, disappearing into the greyish sky.

Zena shivered.

Johnno shook his head in disbelief. "What on earth was that?" he said.

James was running after Joe. "Come back, Joe. Come back," he shouted in a blind panic. But the silence of the fields and the trees pressed all around him. He stopped, gasped, leaning his hands on his knees.

Hot tears scalded his cheeks.

"Whatever's the matter?" asked Zena, putting her arm around him.

They walked the rest of the way home in an embarrassed silence. Zena and Johnno were baffled by the morning's strange turn of events. She was convinced she'd seen a sort of alien presence, and she was struck dumb by it. He decided that it had to be some kind of mirage and he pondered how it could have happened.

Mum took one look at her son's face, and the mud on his clothes, and said, "Is this the way you behave when I let you out on your own? Look at the state of you."

"Sorry, Mum."

"Go upstairs, get those things off and get straight into the shower. I'll have some lunch ready for you when you come down – not that you deserve it."

James ran upstairs to his room.

Are you here, Joe?

Same place.

Joe was resting underneath one of James's T-shirts, a little ball of flickering light.

Thank God.

You needn't have worried, James. I'm never going to leave you, you know, not now that I've found you again.

James sat on the bed and began to peel off his clothes. *Do you really mean that?*

'Course.

What are we going to do about Johnno and Zena? They saw you.

Nothing.

But...

Don't worry. Zena'll think she imagined it,

and Johnno will convince himself I was a shooting star.

James smiled. The panic that had gripped him all the way home evaporated as soon as he heard Joe's voice in his head again.

I hated being without you.

Yeah, I know the feeling. Now, are you going to have that shower? I need a good rest after all the energy you've taken out of me. Buzz off, will you?

By the time James appeared in the kitchen in a clean set of clothes, his hair wet, he was ravenous. Mum watched in amusement at the speed with which he devoured the cheese-on-toast. In between spoonfuls of yoghurt, he told her briefly what had happened that morning, leaving out any mention of Joe, of course.

"Well, I've had a nice morning, too. Mrs McNab called in. We had a good old gossip about the old days. She's auditioning for the play next week after school. She wants you to be in it. I do, too."

"OK."

Mum smiled. "You've made up your mind, then?"

"Yeah. I'd like to play one of the ghosts."

"Oh, trust you to pick a part with the most difficult costume! Mrs McNab will expect me to make it for you, you know."

But James could see she was pleased. With Joe's help, he'd be able to do it, he felt sure of that; but only with Joe's help.

"What are you going to do this afternoon?" Mum asked.

"Nothing much. I think I've done enough for one day."

"You look a bit worn out. You're not used to it, are you. That's my fault."

"Oh, Mum..."

"Well, what about if we finished *A Christmas Carol?*"

Mum cleared some clothes from the chair in James's room and sat down with the book on her lap. James lay on the bed, his hands behind his head, and closed his eyes.

Are you going to listen to this, Joe?

What do you think?

"Now, where did we get to? Ah yes, '*Stave IV: The Last of the Spirits*'. Are you ready, James?"

"I'm ready."

" '*The Phantom slowly, gravely, silently approached. When it came near him, Scrooge bent down upon his knee; for in the very air through which this Spirit moved it seemed to scatter gloom and mystery.*

" '*It was shrouded in a deep black garment, which concealed its head, its face, its form, and left nothing visible save one outstretched hand...*

" '*He felt that it was tall and stately when it came beside him, and that its mysterious presence filled him with a solemn dread. He knew no more, for the Spirit neither spoke nor moved.*

" ' "*I am in the presence of the Ghost of Christmas Yet To Come?*" *said Scrooge.*

" '*The Spirit answered not, but pointed onward with its hand...*' "

Scrooge overheard some businessmen he knew talking of the sad, lonely death of someone they used to work with. He saw three people meet in a hovel and scavenge through the last meagre belongings of the dead man.

And then he saw his own dead body and he knew it was his death they were all talking about. The Spirit whisked him to the Cratchits' house where all was sad too, for Tiny Tim had also passed away. Scrooge, horrified by all this, vowed to change his skinflint ways at once so that none of this would happen. The first thing he did when he woke in the present again on that Christmas day was to send a huge turkey to the Cratchits, and he gave Bob a rise. Thereafter "...*it was always said of him, that he knew how to keep Christmas well, if any man alive possessed the knowledge. May that be truly said of us, and all of us! And so, as Tiny Tim observed, God Bless Us, Everyone!*"

"That ghost is the scariest of the three," said James.

"The most mysterious," said Mum, closing the book.

"It must be weird being able to look into the future."

"If only," said Mum quietly. James watched her leave the room, her shoulders hunched.

She's sad, said Joe.

Yeah, because of you.

I couldn't help it.

If you could have seen into the future, though...

Don't think about it, James. It's not like that on the other side. It's all fog and darkness, believe me.

In bed that night, James studied a picture an artist had drawn of the last ghost in *A Christmas Carol.* Joe was hovering, a misty shape, just above him.

Joe, could you change into a shape like that? Could you look like the third ghost?

I could try. It'd take a lot of energy, though.

Try it, will you?

James watched Joe struggling to form the shape of the Spirit. The outline of the hooded figure with outstretched hand came and went, wavering indistinctly.

I can't hold it, Joe gasped, disappointed. *I've used up so much energy on you these past two days, I haven't got enough for this.*

James got out of bed and stood in front of Joe's spirit.

I could give you some of that energy back.

There was a pause. *No, James, you mustn't.*

Only a bit. Like we did before in the flat.

Blue light flickered through Joe. He hesitated. *I mustn't.* But he couldn't help himself. *OK. Just this once.*

James reached out and touched the hand that was still extended from Joe's wavering form. A blue current fizzed fiercely between them. The force of it knocked James back on to the bed.

Was that enough? he gasped.

But he need not have asked. Suddenly, there towered before him the dark, hooded, mysterious figure of the Ghost of Christmas Yet To Come. The apparition seemed no longer anything to do with Joe. The glowing red eyes in the Spirit's hood grew large and burnt their way into his mind. He felt afraid. He slid back into bed and pulled the covers up to his face.

Joe? I've had enough. Change back, OK?

The Spirit pointed its bony finger at the boy. *Look now upon thy death, oh wretched boy, and ponder the fate that awaits you.*

Chapter 7

James found it hard to get up next morning. His head felt stuffy, his limbs heavy, the light hurt his eyes. Mum was concerned at how pale he looked and insisted that he stayed in. James didn't mind: he hadn't much energy for anything else. He dozed, played on his computer for a while, read. From time to time he looked into the drawer, lifted a T-shirt, to check that Joe was still there.

Are you asleep, Joe?

Yes.

You scared me last night.

Good.

What do you mean?

That's what I was supposed to do, wasn't I?

You were very real.

Yeah, I felt real. It was great. But I don't think we'd better do it too often, James.

No. I feel like death warmed up today.

You feel what?

Oops! Sorry.

I'm going back to sleep.

But on the Saturday night they did it again; they couldn't resist the excitement of it. This time Joe was the Ghost of Christmas Present. James wasn't afraid of this ghost, but he soon crashed out from loss of energy and fell into a deep sleep.

Joe hovered over him for a while, strangely agitated. James's energy, the energy of life, crackled in him. There was going to be no sleep for him that night.

He changed into the shape of a boy again and drifted through the walls, out into the night. His feet did not quite touch the ground. In the dark and the lamplight, he found that people passing on the other side of the road did not glance at him more than once. It was only those few unfortunates who passed on his side that looked on him and fled.

With a little bit more of James's energy...
No, I mustn't think that way. Never.

Of course I'm coming with you!

It was Monday morning. James, still feeling a bit washed out after Saturday night's energy-exchange, was packing his bag for school.

What if you're discovered?

I'll just zoom off, like I did the other day.

James giggled. *Johnno and Zena will really freak out then!*

On the way to school that morning he no longer had any need to invent conversations with his brother: they never stopped talking. Joe admitted to being a bit nervous, which made James feel uncharacteristically protective towards him.

The whole school went into Assembly.

As soon as the class had gone, Joe changed into the familiar ball of light and began, cautiously, to drift around the school. He kept to the ceiling, dodging behind beams –

it was an old building in parts – and cupboards to avoid detection. The school secretary, staggering down the corridor with a large pile of registers and dinner-money, thought she caught sight of a ball of light floating above her head and nearly dropped her load in amazement.

It felt strange to be back in that school, which he had gone to himself as an infant and first year junior. *I am the Ghost of Christmas Past*, he said to himself, seeing the stack of Dickens' book on Mrs McNab's desk.

As the class filed back into the classroom, Joe lodged himself in the angle where two dusty beams met, high in the ceiling. He looked down on James, who was sitting at a table with Johnno and Zena.

"Settle down," said Mrs McNab, "and get your English books out."

There was a general milling about before she got them settled down again, their pens poised above a clean page headed with the date.

"Now," she said. "Cast your mind back to

last week. I want you to choose one incident from that week – something that happened to you – which you want to share with us. And just to make it a bit more challenging – don't groan, Zena, it doesn't become you – I want you to try and tell it from someone else's point of view."

"What do you mean?" someone asked.

"Well, from your mum's point of view, or a friend's. Whoever was with you. Put yourself in their shoes and tell it as *they* saw it."

Some were intrigued by this idea, some daunted.

James sighed. Why did Mrs MacNab put him through this torture? He would never be able to write more than a few lines. He looked enviously at Johnno, who had already written three lines – "I'm going to write about our day on the river," he said – and at Zena, who was dashing down, in her large, curly handwriting, the first thing that came into her mind. Soon, it seemed, everyone was writing except James.

What's the problem? Joe asked.

I can't spell. And I can't write.

Really? Since when?

Since... Well, you know.

Joe understood. He was appalled. He kept silent for a while.

The trouble is, he said, *I can't really spell, either. I haven't been to school for a while, you see.*

Oh, don't they have schools in Ghostland?

Ghostland!

Just joking.

Well, tell you what. I can see into that big dictionary on Mrs McNab's desk. You tell me what word you want and I'll tell you how to spell it – if I can find it.

So that's what they did. James managed to write six lines about his time at the swimming-baths, told from Zena's point of view. Mrs MacNab was impressed by the spelling; even the handwriting had improved!

But isn't it cheating?

Of course not!

James walked out into the playground feeling rather more confident because of that. Joe, invisible again, floated by his side.

I can feel your coldness.

And I can feel your warmth.

James watched some boys from his year play football. Not being fast enough or skilful enough to control the ball, he'd long ago given up on that game. But that didn't mean that he'd stopped wishing he could play.

Can you help me play football, Joe?

Doubt it, Joe answered with a laugh.

Why not? You used to be good at it.

I can put ideas into your head, James, but I can't control your body.

Not even if you gave me a bit of your energy? Like you did to help me cross that ditch?

Yeah, but that gave you confidence, remember, not skill.

So you won't help me?

I don't think it will work.

Just let me try.

OK. But don't expect miracles.

After lunch, they were choosing teams on the field. James jostled to the front and found himself being chosen to make up the numbers.

You've got to help me, Joe, he said, taking up his position on the wing.

It won't be easy. All I can do is give you advice.

Which was what he did. It helped James to anticipate when the ball was coming his way and where best to position himself, but once he got the ball, he was all feet and legs. It was easy to get the ball off him; and when he did manage to pass it, the kick lacked strength or direction.

"You're useless, Hurrell," was said more than once.

When they changed over ends, James said, *Please help me, Joe. Give me some of your energy.*

OK, Joe sighed.

James reached out and felt Joe's cold, invisible fingers grasp his hand. He shivered for a second or two, and then felt a crackle of energy flow into his limbs.

Now he was full of confidence and courage, tackling the toughest players with little fear, hurtling about with the ball as if a pack of demons was after him. But still he lacked the skill, still his passes went wild, his kicks far of the mark. He fell over too often and nearly scored an own-goal. Towards the end, half the players and spectators were looking at him in amazement, the other half were in stitches.

Joe kept quiet. He knew this was likely to happen and he wanted his brother to learn a lesson from it. He couldn't go on giving James his energy, it was costing him too much. But he watched his brother closely, and as the minutes ticked by, envy crept back into him. Envy that his brother was alive, out there playing with his school-mates, while he had to stay insubstantial and alone, unseen. *As if I don't exist. It isn't fair.*

Just before home time, Mrs McNab announced, "Tomorrow, after school, in Drama Club, I shall be auditioning for the Christmas play. Anyone who wants to be in it should tell their parents they will be late. Make up your minds which parts you want to play, but have more than one in mind, please, in case you don't get your first choice. And no time-wasters. This is going to be a classy production and I only want people in it who are really keen."

James shivered with anticipation. *I'll be in it if you'll help me, Joe. I can't do it on my own.*

I'll be there. I know something about playing the part of a ghost, remember?

The feeling of envy persisted in Joe for the rest of the day. He knew it was a dangerous and unfair emotion, but it was like a dull, sickly light inside him which he could not put out.

About midnight, when James was asleep, he touched his brother and felt the boy's live, warm energy flow into him. *I'm only taking back what I gave him today*, he said to himself. But he took much more than that: he couldn't help himself. Then he changed into the shape of a boy. He looked at himself in the mirror: he was almost lifelike. Still the pallor, still the faint phosphorescent glow, still the opaque eyes, but otherwise... He shivered with guilty excitement. *Sorry, James,* he said, waving to his sleeping brother from the door.

Then he was out, walking the night streets.

A late-night film was just over and a small crowd was spilling on to the street. He positioned himself in their path, so that they had to walk around him. Few people gave him a glance, and probably only did so because he seemed too young to be out at that hour.

He smiled triumphantly to himself. *No one knew he was a ghost. They thought he was alive!* Was this the way out of the dark limbo he was in? Was this his way back to life?

Chapter 8

"I'm not sure you should be going to school looking like that," Mum said, concerned at James's pallor and the shadows under his eyes.

"I'm all right, Mum, really," he yawned, although he felt far from it. His eyelids were heavy, his head was stuffy, his limbs were sluggish. "It's the auditions for the play today. I can't miss them."

"But you're so pale. Look at him, Donald. You're not going to tell me there's nothing wrong with him?"

Dad didn't want to be drawn into this. He had a busy day of meetings ahead of him; he had no time to worry about his son. But he made an effort. "How do you feel really, James?"

"Just a bit tired. Must have been that football match yesterday."

"Oh, you played football?" said Dad.

"Yeah, it was great, although I didn't score. Our team won though."

"And you want to go today?"

"Yeah."

"Good lad."

Mum sighed. "Well, the school knows where to contact me. Just promise me you'll get them to ring if you don't feel well."

"Promise," James mumbled. He was fed up being treated like a kid. As bad as he felt – and he *did* feel bad – he was determined he'd get through the day as normal.

"Good luck with the auditions," said Dad at the front door. "Give it all you've got."

Joe was feeling remorse. He knew he had done wrong in drawing energy from James the previous night, but he did not want to admit it.

I'm not coming with you today.

James was dismayed. *Why not?*

You mustn't get to rely on me.

But I don't.

That's what was happening yesterday.

Yeah, but I wouldn't do it every day.

You wouldn't be able to resist. I know I wouldn't in the same situation.

Oh, please, Joe. I won't be able to do the auditions if you don't come.

You could, if you really tried.

No, James scowled. *You know that's not true. If you don't help me — if we don't do this together — I shan't get the parts. I just know it.*

OK. I'll meet you at the school in time for the auditions.

After school? But how will you get there?

How do you think?

You'll have to be careful, Joe. What if you're seen?

A few people will be puzzled, that's all. Now, let me sleep. I'll see you later.

James had the sensation of a switch going off in his mind. *Joe? Are you there? Why don't you answer me?* But there was no answer. This was the first time his brother had 'switched off'.

James sat silent in the car as Mum drove him to school. He was troubled by the sudden break in the telepathy with his brother. Something was wrong with his brother... Something was wrong with them both.

Mrs McNab could see that he was not well. She gave him an easy time during the day, letting him stay in during break and lunchtime. He even had a short nap in the tiny sickroom. Mrs McNab was all for calling Mum but he begged her not to.

The bell went for home time and all the children left except for the dedicated band who gathered in the hall for the auditions.

Where was Joe?

Mrs McNab had taken them all for drama many times before: they were used to her methods. She did not believe in using written scripts. Anyone who was in a play directed by her had to make up their own dialogue. "Much more interesting for everyone," she declared. "Much more educational. Scripts make everyone sound like automata."

"Or – what?" Zena asked.

"Never you mind, Zena. I can be quite confident that that is something you will never resemble!"

"She means a robot," Johnno whispered to her. He had been persuaded, mainly by a very persistent Zena, to take part, and he had his eyes on the character of old Jacob Marley, the first ghost to haunt Scrooge.

For the first half hour, they were allowed to practise parts in little groups around the hall. Mrs McNab observed them all, jotting down on a clipboard who was going to audition for each part.

Meanwhile, Joe had set out for the school in good time, as a hovering ball of light, but he saw so many things on the way that roused his interest – and his mortal memories – that he kept stopping to observe. He managed to keep hidden from most eyes, although a few people stared at him as he floated past. It amused him to see the startled expression, on their faces. What did they make of him? Was he an alien? An illusion? A UFO?

By the time he arrived at the school, James

was already in the middle of his audition for the Ghost of Christmas Past.

His brother was making a hash of it. James was not only feeling unwell, he was unnerved by the apparent desertion of his brother. He had started off fairly well, improvising the first meeting between himself and Scrooge, but once they started on the journey through scenes from the old miser's past, he got confused.

"I know you're supposed to be a ghost, James, but put at least a little life into it."

James struck a few poses and tried to look awesome. Zena giggled.

"And speak up, we can hardly hear you."

James immediately became tongue-tied. He was always inclined to stammer when unsure of himself, and he felt the words begin to scramble on his tongue.

Then, with enormous relief, he heard Joe's voice in his head.

Sorry I'm late, Bruv. How's it going?

Terrible. Help me.

How? You know the story as well as I do.

Let me touch you. Give me energy.

OK. But I wish I could take your place. I'd be convincing!

Yeah, James scowled. *You needn't rub it in.*

"James?" called Mrs McNab. "Are you all right?"

"Yes. Can I just go out and get a drink?"

"Go on, then. We'll come back to your scene. Let's move on to the scene with Mrs Cratchit – is that you, Zena? – and her family cooking the Christmas lunch."

In the cloakroom, James felt Joe's cold energy course through him, lifting the heaviness from his limbs and the stuffiness from his head. Suddenly, he felt light and clear. *I shall know what to say now*, he said.

Mrs McNab marvelled at the sudden change in him. What a strange boy he was turning out to be.

Joe watched him attack his part with new energy. He could see that everyone was watching him now with real interest. They all sensed that something had happened in the few minutes that he had been out of the hall, that he had suddenly got hold of the part. Envy began to throb in Joe again. It was *his* energy, *his* confidence, that was making this happen. If only...

How did I do, Joe?

You were great. You'll get the part.

You think so?

I know so. I can see Mrs McNab writing it down.

I couldn't have done it without you.

No, of course not.

Are you all right, Joe? You sound...

Yeah, I'm fine. Don't worry about me.

Mrs McNab looked at her watch. "Goodness, is that the time? We haven't got through half the auditions yet. Can everyone meet again on Thursday after school? We've got to get this sorted out as soon as we can."

"Can I try for the part of the other two ghosts?" James asked eagerly.

Mrs McNab looked at her clipboard. "Fiona's put down for the second and third ghosts, so you'll have some competition, but I don't see why not, James. You did the first ghost surprisingly well towards the end. Let's see how you get on."

James felt so buoyed up by this first success, he chatted all the way home about it, about how he was going to tackle the next two ghosts and beat Fiona. He didn't think about Joe's silence, he just assumed his brother was happy at his success. And of course, Joe was; but there were other, stronger, darker emotions struggling for expression inside the ghost of James's twin.

Joe was rediscovering what it was like to be a boy again, at least a night-time boy, after years of being little more than a cold mist, lost in a world between life and death. But to be that boy, he had to take vital energy from his brother: temptation stared him in the face. Conscience stopped him from going out on that Tuesday night, but having slept all Wednesday, he could not resist it again and took to the streets in the small hours.

James felt groggy again on Thursday, but he wouldn't admit it even to his mother.

Please come with me, he said to Joe. *It was horrible yesterday without you.*

At school, Joe watched his brother from his vantage point between the ceiling beams. He helped him with a spelling test. *Twenty out of twenty, Joe! I've never done that before.* He helped him beat Johnno at chess. He was intrigued by a science experiment that kept his brother busy in a group all afternoon. And envy – a longing to be alive, to be down there, a *real* boy – built up inside him until he felt he would burst. When the bell went for home time, he had had enough.

I'm going home, James.

What? Why? We've got the audition next.

I can't help it. I've got to go.

Why?

Why do you think? Joe said, suddenly bitter.

James was baffled.

I'll see you back home.

But Joe...

Bye, James. Good luck with the Ghost of Christmas Present.

Joe, please come back.

But Joe was already drifting away, passing

through the classroom wall and into the playground.

James ran outside. He stood in the playground and shouted to Joe to come back.

"James?" said Mrs McNab, coming out to see what the matter was. She saw the deep, troubled scowl on his face. "Whatever is it?"

"Nothing," he mumbled, keeping his head down.

"Who were you shouting for?" Had she really heard him shouting his dead brother's name?

"Nobody."

"Well, if you've finished shouting for Mr Nobody, are you going to come to the audition? You did the Ghost of Christmas Past very well on Tuesday, after you got going."

James just wanted to give up the whole idea. He'd been feeling lousy all day, and now that Joe had inexplicably deserted him... But the will to do it, and the expectant look in his teacher's eyes, persuaded him to step back inside.

It was no good, though. His performance

was confused, wooden, hesitant. He forgot the story, couldn't think what to say, stammered.

Fiona had secured the parts in the second act that she had wanted. Now she, too, tried for the Ghost of Christmas Present. It didn't seem quite right, a girl playing the part, but as no other boy wanted to do it – Johnno refused to be in competition with James – she was "pencilled in", as Mrs McNab put it, for the part. James was devastated.

James trudged straight up to his room.

Joe knew immediately that things hadn't gone well. *What happened?*

I made a mess of it, that's what happened.

But why?

You know why.

Do I?

You shouldn't have left me. I couldn't do it without you. Fiona's got the part now. What am I going to tell Mum? Dad?

I'm sorry.

Why did you go?

Because I thought you didn't need me.

You knew I needed you. Why?

Joe was on the point of telling him, but he drew back. *I've told you.*

James sensed the evasion: doubt and distrust grew in his mind. While he changed out of his school uniform, into jeans and a sweatshirt, he felt angry emotions bubbling up inside him.

Don't say it, Joe said, alarmed.

But James ignored him. *You're jealous, aren't you. Jealous of me, because I'm alive. Because I can do things.*

This was so near the mark, Joe forced himself to keep quiet.

That's why you wanted me to fail the audition.

James opened the drawer in which Joe was hiding. *Well, why don't you say something?*

Joe tried to keep back the words, but when James slammed the drawer in disgust, something snapped inside him. He emerged from the drawer, broke free of the globe of light and shimmered into the blurred form of a boy. He flickered with sudden anger.

Yes, all right, I am jealous! he hissed,

startling James with the aggression in his voice. *Is it so surprising? Think about it! I hate being invisible, as if I'm not really there. I hate having to do everything through you. I hate having to hide, to run away, not to be able to do what I want. Can you imagine what it is like watching you make a mess of the auditions, when I know I could do it ten times better than anyone else? Or watching you play football? Never to be seen, never to be touched, never to be alive? Can you possibly imagine what it's like? Of course you can't! You only ever think of yourself.*

If James had sympathized then, everything might have been smoothed over, but he couldn't, he was still feeling too sore about being let down by his brother. He hadn't heard half of what Joe had said.

So you spoil it for me, then, eh? said James. *What sort of brother would do that?*

Come on! Trust you to see it like that.

You thought, if you can't do it, then I won't either.

That's not fair! I've been helping you all day.

That gave James pause for thought. He

turned away and looked out of the window. *Then why didn't you help me at the audition? You knew I'd make a mess of it.*

I didn't do it on purpose. Come on, I...

I don't believe you.

There was a troubled silence. James's mood was growing darker. Joe was trying to hold back his anger.

Look, James, I'm not sure all this is a good idea.

What isn't?

Me and you.

Why? I don't understand you. Why are you being so horrible?

I'm not. You just think I am.

Of course you are.

Joe had had enough. *Oh, I give up.* He turned away, shimmering in frustration and disgust.

James couldn't help himself either. "Well, if being a ghost is so horrible when you're with me," he shouted, turning towards the door, "why don't you just go away, then? Find someone else to be with." With a final twist, he added, "I was all right until you came."

He left the room, slamming the door behind him, and went down to the sitting-room. There he sat, hunched and smouldering, in front of the television.

Gradually, as James sat there in troubled thought, as he forced down his dinner and struggled with his homework, his anger and disappointment died down, leaving only fatigue and sadness. He began to see Joe's point of view. He began to regret their row and his parting shot. He wanted to go up and say he was sorry, that he didn't mean what he had said, but for a long time pride and timidity kept him glued to his seat. But then a sudden fear assailed him. He ran up to his bedroom.

Joe? I'm sorry if... Joe?

The room was silent, empty. James hurriedly opened the drawer where Joe usually hid. He wasn't there.

Joe, where are you?

His voice echoed in his head. There was no answer.

James kept awake half the night, waiting for Joe's return.

Please, Joe, please. Come back. I didn't mean what I said...

In the morning, there was still no sign of his brother. Joe had taken him at his word. Joe had left him.

Pleading illness, James refused to go to school that Friday. He stayed in bed, brooding on yesterday's sudden, unexpected, horrible row. Gradually, he understood how his brother must be feeling, and he blamed himself bitterly for it. *I didn't mean it, Joe. Come back*, he said over and over again, hoping for a response.

But none came.

Chapter 9

I *was all right until you came.*

Those words had really stung Joe. His brother could not have said a more hurtful thing. The fact that there was some truth in it only made it worse. Joe writhed, hurt and angry, until he knew that he could no longer stay with his brother.

He hovered briefly above the house. He could see James hunched in front of the television. *So that's how much all this means to him*, he thought bitterly, and he sped off into the darkening sky.

By nightfall, he was back in the derelict flat. It was even more desolate now than before his meeting with James.

He brooded. He could not, would not, go back to the lonely life as it was before he had made contact with his brother. And he had tasted life again: he needed his brother for that. He would have to visit James secretly at night and draw energy from him. It would tire James, even make him ill at times perhaps, but was that so bad after all that James had said?

But later, with the moon slowly invading the room, he had a new idea. Why just take on the shape of the boy he had once been in life? Why just draw energy from James? Couldn't he just as easily draw energy from someone else and assume *their* shape? At first the idea seemed to hold some hidden danger, and he tried to dismiss it, but it persisted.

By morning, he felt, in desperation, he should give it a try.

He floated above the houses and streets, looking for someone to make contact with. A milkman? A paperboy? A woman shopper? No, it had to be... *Ah, now this looks promising.* In the forecourt of a block of garages, a young motorcyclist, wearing goggles, was wheeling out a big, black, gleaming motorbike from a garage. He wore black leather from head to foot. *Yes! Imagine being him!*

Swiftly, Joe descended and materialized as a boy. He had not enough energy to become solid, so that his shape wavered and was semi-transparent at times. The motorcyclist, who was about to put on his crash-helmet, paused and stared in amazement; then his helmet crashed to the ground.

"Don't be afraid," said Joe. He had not used his voice before – it sounded like air blown through a pipe, deep but reedy and hoarse – and he giggled at the sound of it. "I just want you to touch me."

Joe held out his hand and stepped closer to the motorcyclist. The youth stepped back, removed his goggles, then froze. The blood drained from his face.

"Hold out your hand," Joe demanded, reaching out.

Involuntarily, the motorcyclist raised his hand, perhaps to obey, perhaps to ward off the apparition. Their fingertips touched. Currents of blue energy hissed between them. The motorcyclist staggered back with a cry until he was forced against the garage door. Joe moved with him to maintain the current.

The man fainted, crumpling to the ground, and the current ceased.

Joe concentrated all his new-found energy on changing his shape. Within a minute he had become identical to the motorcyclist, except for the usual tell-tale signs: the slight glow of his pallid skin, the opaque eyes, the chill in the air around him.

Fantastic!

He looked briefly at the motorcyclist. He'd be all right after a good sleep.

He took a few steps and then saw himself in the motorcycle's wing mirror. The sight gave him a shock. He stared and stared. *He was someone else*. How strange that looked. That felt.

As he walked out of the courtyard, the balls of his feet not quite touching the ground, he kept thinking, *I'm not Joe any more, I'm someone else. I'm someone I don't know. Someone else!*

A minute later, in the street around the corner, a woman suddenly came out of a doorway, setting off for work. "Oh, Jake," she said to him, surprised. "Haven't you gone yet? You'll be late."

She came towards him. The smile froze on her face. "Jake, are you all right? You look..." She stared at Joe's seemingly sightless eyes, she felt the chill waves coming from him, and she faltered. "Jake, what's the matter? *What's happened to you?*"

Joe felt foolish. He raised his hand.

The woman screamed. She turned back to her house, frantically inserted the key, and fled inside, banging the door behind her.

Joe shivered.

Was everyone turning against him?

As he walked the streets and wandered into shops and stores, he was aware of the quizzical looks he was getting. His eyes, his skin, the atmosphere around him... Slowly, he began to admit that he could not, in broad daylight, pass for a real human. Not really.

But worse than that was the strange transformations that seemed to be happening inside him. These were far more scary. His own identity as Joe seemed to be shrinking, curling up into a tighter and tighter ball under the pressure of the new thoughts, the new identity, he had taken on. Suddenly, as he stood on a traffic island in the middle of a busy street, a terrifying thought flashed through him: *I'm turning into someone else.*

The thought was such a shock, he stepped out unthinkingly into the road, into the path of an oncoming car. Someone shouted, "Look out!" There was a shriek of brakes. The driver closed his eyes. Eyewitnesses stared in horror. But what they saw staggered them. *The car passed right through him.* When it came to a halt, Joe was behind it, still walking in a daze across the road.

He reached the pavement. The wildness of people's looks scared him. He ran away from them, gliding over the pavement as if on rollerblades. Shouts to come back faded away.

No, it was going to be impossible to be accepted, even in disguise.

He found a mirror in a clothes shop and stared at himself. A youth with a white face and strange eyes, sheathed in black leather.

Who was he? Joe? Or this strange new personality called Jake?

He looked like Jake. Jake's thoughts and feelings were noisily crowding his mind now. Joe was being stifled.

"Can I help you, Sir?" an attendant asked. He blanched when Joe turned to face him, when he saw the seemingly sightless eyes.

"No," said Joe in sudden despair. "No one can."

He hurried back out into the street and walked and walked in a turmoil of thought – until he knew what he had to do.

He sped back to the garage courtyard. The motorcyclist and the motorbike had gone.

He had to find Jake. Jake's thoughts, Jake's feelings, Jake's memories, were pressing so hard now on his own sense of self, he knew he might soon be overwhelmed by them, caving in like a crushed egg.

He rose and floated over the neighbouring houses, looking through the roofs and walls. There were so many.

Jake was filling him with anger now,

flooding him. Joe was being drowned in the noise, the feeling.

I must find him... There isn't much time left.

Then he saw the woman he had encountered earlier: she was sitting by Jake in a bedroom, holding his hand while he slept. Of course, why hadn't he gone straight to that house? Joe wished she wasn't there, but there was no time to wait for her to leave. He descended through the roof and ceiling into the bedroom and stood beside the bed. The woman leapt up and shrank back. What was she seeing? She looked, with frightened, swivelling eyes, from Jake to the ghost and back again. Fear made her sway on her feet. Had he died? Was this his spirit?

Joe ignored her. He touched Jake's hand and the blue current fizzed between them. Joe willed all the stolen energy back into Jake. He felt Jake's personality flow out of him, drain out of him like liquid from an upturned bottle.

His own personality broke from its confines and filled the emptiness. At last he was himself again. The relief was enormous.

Changing swiftly into the familiar ball of light, he sped away. He left the woman looking down in relief and astonishment as her boyfriend woke from his slumber.

Joe understood then. He could only be himself with James. That's what being two halves of the same being meant. *Really* meant. He hadn't realized that before. Not fully.

He settled down in the corner of the room in the deserted flat, where their bunk beds used to be, and curled up to sleep, a vague, misty boy-shape, softly luminous in the shadows.

On Saturday James felt even worse. There was a sadness in the pit of his stomach as heavy as stone. How could he have said those things? How could he have driven away his brother with such horrible, hurtful words? What was the matter with him?

Mum came in with a late breakfast. "That was Zena on the phone. I said you won't be coming out today."

He nodded.

She put down the tray. "Do you have a headache?"

He shook his head.

"All the same..." she said, looking doubtful.

He realized then that she was debating whether to take him to the doctor's. "I'm all right, Mum, really. Just tired."

Dad, poking his head in, said, "Too much football, eh?"

"Yeah," James answered, managing a grin.

"And those rehearsals, too, I should think," Mum added. She'd been talking to Mrs McNab on the phone.

"I'm going down to the garden centre later on," said Dad. "Do you think you'll be up to coming?"

James nodded. He didn't want to go anywhere, but he knew it would only make things worse if his parents started getting really worried about him. Especially Mum.

Being outside and with Dad made him feel a bit better; it made him feel normal, at least outwardly. He helped Dad in the garden in the afternoon, clearing up leaves, piling up pruned twigs, planting bulbs. But as dusk fell and the air grew chill, desolation crept up on him.

"You've over-tired him," Mum complained when he and Dad came in. And it was true, he felt exhausted. He had a bath, then watched television, forcing down a sandwich Mum had made for him. He felt as fragile as a shell, the ache in the pit of his stomach beginning to hurt.

Please come back, Joe. Please...

The night was full of tossing and turning. Words echoed and stung in the darkness.

He woke very early: it was still dark. He'd dreamt again of the time before the accident, the time in the flat. A thought flashed through him: That's where Joe must be. That's where he'd find his brother. He sat up in the semi-darkness. Should he go there? Now?

The moon was still bright in the strange, lurid grey light of the morning. James pulled his jacket tightly around him and hurried, head down, as fast as he could through the narrow, shadowy streets. When he arrived at the derelict flats, he was out of breath and trembling. What he saw then made him draw up sharp. The wire fence that had been around the flats had been removed. Other derelict buildings nearby had been demolished: all that was left of them were shadowy piles of broken bricks and concrete. The flats were the last standing. He had come just in time.

The boards covering the main entrance had been broken open. He could step through the gap into the dank vestibule, just as he used to. He groped his way up the dark stairs until he reached the flat door.

Such a strange sense of *déjà vu* over came him then: from the past, from a fortnight ago, he couldn't tell. He ran along the hall and into their old bedroom.

Joe, glowing softly in the dark, was curled up asleep on the floor where the bunk beds used to be. *Thank God*, James said, leaning against the windowsill and taking gulps of breath.

Calming a little, he crept close to his brother and watched the light flicker faintly over the surface of his ghostly clothes. As he watched, the sight of this insubstantial form was replaced by a memory so vivid, so bright and clear, of his brother as he was in life, he smiled and reached out. Before, when they had fallen out, they had made up at night by curling up, wordless, in the same bunk together. James felt himself slipping back into the past. Not caring what he might be doing, he stretched out beside his brother. Cold enveloped him. He felt Joe stirring. He felt Joe's chilly embrace.

Dimly, through a swirl of mist, he saw Joe's face close to him, coming closer until he was a blur. He heard Joe whisper something in his head. It was a faint warning, but he did not heed it. He did not struggle. Cold and darkness folded into him. He had the sensation of drifting through space with no light, not even a star.

Wake up, James, wake up.

He stirred. Feeling cold, he reached for his duvet. There was nothing there. He opened his eyes and struggled into a sitting position. Pale sunlight filtered through the grimy windows.

I shan't ask how you feel. I know!

Joe felt so close, closer than he had ever been before. *Where are you?*

Here, Joe answered with a chuckle. His voice was clearer and stronger than James had ever known it — like the difference between listening to music from speakers and listening to it through earphones.

James looked round. *Where?*

Joe chuckled again. *Can't you guess?*

Something was different deep inside him. The ache had gone, the sadness, the guilt at turning his brother away... No, it was more than that. Much more. A fullness — how could he put it?

He looked down to where he had slept and then remembered how he had curled up with his brother, just as they had when Joe had been alive. A thought so startling entered his head, he jumped up and shook himself and tried to push it away. He went to the window and looked out over the rooftops to the river glinting through the Common. The thought flooded back. *Joe,* he said in trepidation, *it feels like you're... you're...*

Inside you?

Inside him! That was it!

Yeah! Not just your voice, but all of you. Like I'm two beings.

Yeah. Something weird happened last night. You did what I told you never to do – you touched me all over. There was a fusion of energy: light and dark, cold and warmth, life and death. Our defences were down and we merged. It happened before I could stop it. I was drawn into you. In the end, you see, the living are stronger than the dead.

James clutched his head in his hands and paced up and down the bare boards, trying to get hold of this incredible idea. *Inside me? Not just your voice but your whole being?*

That's right.

For a long time James stood, swaying slightly on his heels, his eyes closed, his attention turned inwards. He could not see Joe but he felt him everywhere inside him. And his brother was warm – not the cold, misty presence he had always been as a ghost, but something living and breathing. Not an invasion, either, but a comfortable co-existence, like their curling up together in bed. He stopped swaying. Happiness began to trickle into him, then flooded like a burst of light. He stopped swaying and opened his eyes.

See? said Joe.

Do you mind?

Mind? Are you kidding? It's the best thing that's happened to me! We're truly together again. This time for ever.

For ever?

Yes, I think so. I don't see how this process can be reversed.

You don't think you can leave me? My body?

I don't know. Perhaps. But right now that's the last thing I want to do.

Same here.

OK. What shall we do now?

I'm taking you home, said James.

No you're not.

I'm not? What do you mean?

We're going home. We make decisions together now, OK?

OK, said James with a laugh.

Chapter 10

James managed to get back home that morning without being missed. When his parents heard him downstairs, they assumed he had just got up.

"Make us some tea, will you, James," Dad shouted at him from the landing.

It was the last thing James felt like doing at that moment. *Act normal*, said Joe.

Easier said than done. James couldn't organize himself. He forgot to turn on the kettle, he broke the handle on a mug, he put too much tea in the pot and had to start again. Did Mum take sugar? *Of course she does, even I remember that*, Joe said, amused by the effect he was having on his brother.

As he caught sight of himself in the landing mirror, the tray wobbled unsteadily in his hands. His eyes glittered a bit, and there was a strange, twitchy look on his pale face.

"Well, done, lad," Dad muttered. "Has the paper arrived yet?"

James felt Mum's eyes on him. "How do you feel this morning, James?"

"Oh, much better," he answered, aware that Mum was watching the tremble in his hands as he put down the tray on the dresser.

Oh, boy, this is weird, said Joe. *I can't take this.*

In the past, Sunday mornings had been a special time for them. They had romped about the bed, or they had squeezed between their parents demanding a story.

I'm too old for that! James said.

"You got up early," Mum observed, reaching over to pour the tea.

"Back to his old self again, I should think," said Dad.

James, can we leave now? This is making me so sad, I could scream.

OK.

James felt almost the same himself. To have two voices inside him, two personalities, however close they were, made him jumpy, to say the least.

He could settle to nothing that morning. Breakfast turned to sawdust in his mouth. Television programmes didn't make sense. He laughed insanely at a perfectly ordinary photograph of the queen on the front of the newspaper. He ran up and down stairs on the slightest excuse, often forgetting why by the time he reached his room.

His parents watched him with increasing amazement.

"Have you got ants in your pants?" asked Mum

"Worms, more like," said Dad.

"Don't be disgusting," said James.

Weird, said Joe for the umpteenth time.

"Well, you've certainly perked up," said Mum, suspiciously. "But I wish you hadn't perked up quite so much."

The morning was punctuated with, "Don't keep thumping up and down those stairs, James." Or, "Slow down, we haven't got a train to catch." Or, "Now look what you've done! Whatever's got into you this morning?"

By lunchtime Mum's patience had snapped and he was sent to his room to cool down.

This is your doing, Joe.

Our doing, you mean.

Yeah. The thought of you inside me... It's incredible! It makes me feel like... like...

A cat on a hot tin roof!

Right!

They went for a walk that afternoon, all three – or four – of them.

"I've heard that the flats are coming down today," Dad said at the lunch table. "I've been wanting to see them come down ever since we moved out."

"Let's go then, Dad."

"Janice? Do you want to come?"

Mum looked at Dad, a flicker of panic in her eyes. James and Joe waited in suspense. *Say yes*, said Joe. "Go on, Mum," James said softly.

She looked away, sighed, then got up to take the dishes out into the kitchen.

Dad winked at James.

"OK," she said, when she returned. "I suppose we'd all like to see them come down."

Too right, said Joe.

"Too right," echoed James, bursting into uncontrollable laughter.

A huge ball swung back and forth, crashing into the crumbling brickwork. James had hoped they would dynamite the building, so that he would see it sink rapidly into a sudden cloud of dust, but the flats were not big enough for that.

This is more satisfying, said Joe. *I want to see it taken apart piece by piece.*

The ball got nearer and nearer to the windows of their old flat.

"Remember the parachutes, Dad?" said James.

"You bet," said Dad.

He felt Mum take hold of his hand.

The ball smashed into their flat. The windows caved in.

Thank God I came this morning, Joe.

Yeah, I wonder where I would have gone if you hadn't.

Would you ever have come back?

No.

That shocked James.

Really? Why not?

Because I realized I was bad for you.

I don't believe that.

I was getting jealous. I would have grown to hate you. I wasn't going to let that happen.

And now? You won't get jealous now?

Of course not. Everything's changed now. We're one person.

Two halves...

Of the same person. That's what it feels like.

The flats finally succumbed to the giant ball. Dust settled on a heap of rubble.

"I'm glad I saw that," said Mum, wiping dust, or a tear, from her eye.

Could James sleep? Could he get himself organized in the morning? Could he behave at school? The excitement of having Joe inside him would not let go, it bubbled up all the time, giving him no peace. "You're up in the air all the time," Mum complained, puzzled and amused by this strange change in her son.

Mrs McNab was having the same trouble with him too. His behaviour was appalling: suddenly he was the centre of attention, larking about, cracking jokes, clumsily upsetting things. He wandered out of the classroom without permission, he volunteered for every job, he completed nothing, he hared around the playground like one possessed... "He's gone hyperactive on me," Mrs McNab complained to the headteacher. "I can't do anything with him." On the other hand, his work improved in an equally startling way. Instead of three lines of badly spelt writing, he now did pages and pages with barely a spelling mistake. Stranger still, his handwriting had completely changed, had become huge and untidy, but that was a small price to pay. And his hand was always shooting up with the right answers, he was full of good ideas...

"He's really come out of himself," Mrs McNab had to admit.

Of course, she was on the phone to Mum that Monday evening, and the two women compared notes. They ended up laughing over it: at least this was an improvement on the sad, hesitant boy that James had become.

Zena was delighted by the change. She accepted it almost at once, grateful that there was now someone else in class who was more exuberant, more scatty, than she was. She spent most of that Monday and Tuesday giggling into her hand.

Johnno was put out. He could find no explanation for this "personality change" as he called it; it made him feel uncomfortable. He watched James secretly all the time, turning theories over in his mind to account for the change, but never coming anywhere near the truth.

At lunch time, James hurtled about the football field.

Slow down, James, think what you're doing with the ball.

I don't know what to do with it. That's why I was never any good at football.

OK. Let me take over. I'll show you what to do.

James felt Joe invade his own half and take over his thoughts, his movements. Suddenly, he was playing football like the other boys, keeping control of the ball, making cool decisions. At the end of the match, several boys who had hardly spoken to him before, came up to congratulate him.

That was great, Joe. We really played a good game there.

Yeah, we make a good team, don't we?

By the end of the week, they had both calmed down, much to everyone but Zena's relief. And as the weeks leading up to Christmas ticked by, people noticed a new poise and confidence in James. He was no longer the shy, stammering boy who always said no to everything and followed in others' footsteps. He had his own opinions now, and was not afraid to give them. He seemed to fizz with ideas in art, in science, in writing.

He tackled anyone in games. He was no longer useless in PE. He got into trouble, too, frequently, for talking when he shouldn't, for hitting back when picked upon, for careless and untidy behaviour.

He was a normal boy ... except for one thing. People also noticed how, every now and then, his eyes seemed to turn inward, become a little opaque; he seemed to be abstracting himself. "It's as if he's listening to something no one else can hear," said Johnno, who remained intrigued by this change in his friend. Mrs McNab was worried by it, thinking it might indicate an illness such as epilepsy, but whenever she spoke to him in that condition, he looked up at her and smiled, perfectly normal again. She mentioned it to Mum, who said she'd noticed the same thing, and they agreed to keep an eye on it.

But in the event, that inward-looking gradually faded out. James got so used to having Joe's personality inside him, he no longer kept comparing it to his own. That was the signal that their two halves, already so well linked, were beginning to merge.

James and Joe continued to talk to each other, but increasingly the voices became the same, their thoughts reflected each other's, the silences, grown of accord, grew longer. Joe's sense of fun and daring mingled with James's timidity and sensitivity... All this happened imperceptibly, so that neither was really aware that they were slowly becoming one personality, a balance of them both.

Occasionally, James would say, *Are you still there, Joe?*

Faintly: *Yeah. Are you?*

Of course I am.

Just wondered. It's hard to tell the difference these days.

Yeah, well, don't hold your breath.

What do you mean?

You'll see.

Joe?

Yeah?

Is your voice getting fainter?

No. You're getting deaf!

For the rest of November they continued to rehearse twice a week after school. Mum made a magnificent costume for the Ghost of Christmas Past. At the dress rehearsal in the first week of December, Mrs McNab and the rest of the cast were so impressed with James's performance, it made them take their own parts more seriously. How did he create that sense of foreboding, that glow in his eye, that breath of chill in the air? How did he manage to become so awesome?

Everyone knew that Fiona's performance as the two other ghosts was feeble in comparison to James's. He felt quite sorry for her. She stuck to the same words and actions doggedly throughout, and her costumes weren't up to much either. Mrs McNab would have loved to have given James – the new James – back the parts, but she knew she couldn't. The best she could do was make him their understudy.

James tried to coach Johnno in the role of the ghost of old Jacob Marley, but his friend remained stolid and slightly comical throughout.

"How do you make your eyes go dull like

that? And your face go so white?" said Johnno. "It gives me the shivers."

James just grinned knowingly.

"And you're so cold. I don't understand it."

James had been tempted more than once to tell Johnno and Zena what had been happening to him. After all, they had once seen Joe as a hovering ball of light over a field. Once or twice, too, he had begun to do so, but he could tell by the looks on their faces that they thought he was making it up. He soon gave up. *They'd never understand, anyway*, said Joe faintly. *Who would?*

A week before the first performance, a 'flu bug swept through the ranks of the school, thinning out the numbers in class. There was a strange excitement in the air: who would go down with it next? Whose chair would be empty next day?

Several of the cast were affected. Mrs McNab was in despair. Zena, on whom no 'flu bug could make an impression, excitedly volunteered to take on extra parts – she had been secretly understudying practically every part but the ghosts! Johnno, too, was reluctantly pressed to take the part of Bob Cratchit. And when, on the day before the performance, Fiona's dad came into the classroom and said she'd gone down with it, all eyes turned to James, who grinned ecstatically the minute he closed the door behind him.

"Well," said Mrs McNab. "Think you can handle the other two ghosts without making a fool of yourself this time?"

"Of course."

"Good," she said. She had no doubts on that score this time. "I'll ring your mum about the costumes. Maybe we'll be able to borrow Fiona's."

Because of the 'flu bug, the audience was smaller than had been expected, but there was still a good crowd, wrapped in their coats, waiting expectantly for the stage curtain to open. James's mum and dad sat near the front.

"I'm sure Fiona's costumes won't fit him properly," Mum said. She'd been worrying about this ever since she'd heard the news. James, however, had always brushed the fear aside, almost as if he didn't care. "She's a big girl. James might look lost in her costume, look silly."

"I don't suppose it matters," said Dad. "Don't ghosts wear long, baggy gowns anyway?"

Mum shook her head doubtfully.

"Are you sure you're up to it?" she had asked James after Mrs McNab's phone call with the news. Mrs McNab had had no doubts, but then she was in rather a desperate position.

"Don't you worry, Mum. I know all the words and what to do. I'm the understudy, remember."

She wanted to believe him, but the habit of always worrying about him was still strong. After much more of this anxious questioning, James had said a curious thing. He had risen to leave the room. At the door, he'd said, or she thought he'd said, "Anyway, Joe's with me now. I can do anything." What had he meant by that?

Dad gave her a reassuring smile. He knew that she was really worrying about how James would perform. He was feeling nervous for his son himself. "He'll be all right. I might not have said that a few weeks ago, but now..."

"Yes, of course," she said, relaxing a little. The truth was, she had never seen James act in a play. Joe had been in two nativity plays – the memories of those had begun to fade – but no, she said to herself, I mustn't think of Joe tonight. This is James's night.

James, as the Ghost of Christmas Past, reached out a ghostly hand and drew back the curtain around Scrooge's bed.

He wore a white robe, open to the chest and trimmed with fake summer flowers, a shiny belt around his waist, a sprig of holly in his hand, and a wig of long white hair that flowed down his back. He might have looked faintly ridiculous – but no one laughed. The boy playing Scrooge looked genuinely startled. For as the audience leaned forward in their seats, a strange, ghostly light seemed to rise from his head like a wavering beam. And as he moved, light seemed to flicker all over him like a blue shimmer. The stage grew cold, and the cold waves pushed out into the hall, so that, as they watched Scrooge being taken on a tour of his youth, they shivered in their seats and pulled their coats tighter around them.

Mum and Dad shivered most of all. Dad because he felt that for the first time in his life, he was looking at a real ghost, even as he was telling himself it was only the effect of clever lighting. Mum because there was something about all this that reminded her of the ghost of Joe that she had seen on the landing.

The curtain came down on the first act. There were a few seconds of stunned silence, and then the applause swelled enthusiastically.

"That was amazing," said Zena. "How did you make light come from your head?"

"It was the lights, silly," said Johnno, vaguely pointing to a row of stage lights above their heads.

"Yeah, but it was... Weird."

"Well done, James," Mrs McNab said as she hurried past. "I don't know how you did it, but..." and she waved her hands in the air as if to say words were beyond her.

That was brilliant, Joe.

Yeah. Didn't we do well!

We'd better get into Fiona's costume.

What? That thing? No way! I've told you, we're not going on stage in that green sheet with bits of cotton wool stuck on it.

OK, if you've got the energy, we'll do what you want.

It's your energy too. Mostly yours, now.

Of course. But only you can make it happen.

"James," called Mrs McNab. "Do you want any help with your costume?" She was struggling to help Zena wriggle into a wide, flouncy dress.

"Don't worry, Mrs McNab, I'll change in here," he said, pointing to a screened-off area.

He went behind the screen and stripped down to his underwear.

Now close your eyes, said Joe, *and picture the Ghost of Christmas Present.*

He felt a cold envelope of air around him. Opening his eyes, he saw that now he was in a luminous robe of green, a holly wreath on his head glittering with icicles, an old sword sheath hanging from his belt.

Mrs McNab stared at him with her mouth open. "My goodness," she exclaimed, "however did your mum manage that? It's magnificent."

James hurried past her. He didn't want her to examine him too closely.

We're on, said Joe.

He stepped on stage, among piles of Christmas food and drink and decorations, and called Scrooge to look upon him.

The audience looked too. Was that a phosphorescent light all around him, and were there real flames and smoke rising from the torch he held high above Scrooge's trembling old head? But, although uncanny in his movements, in his voice, in the light that surrounded him, this ghost was not so frightening. The power of his kindness drew out Scrooge's stuttering remorse.

"I see a vacant seat," he said, as they stood looking upon the Cratchits' poor but happy Christmas. "In the chimney-corner, and a crutch without an owner, carefully preserved. If these shadows remain unaltered by the Future, Tiny Tim will die."

"No, no," cried Scrooge. "Oh, no, kind Spirit! say he will be spared."

Were the audience applauding Scrooge's change of heart or James's performance? It was impossible to tell. But the clapping went on and on.

"I'm amazed," said Dad.

"*You* are?" said Mum, taking his arm and smiling broadly. "How do you think I feel? It's unbelievable."

James stepped behind the screen backstage and felt the illusion of the costume fade in an instant. He shivered.

Joe, that was brilliant. But I can sense you're tired. Really tired. Are you?

That took it out of me, said Joe in a voice James could hardly hear. *Really. The last of it. You'll have to do the next one, James. On your own. I shall stay silent now.*

James felt troubled by that, but there was no time to think about it. *Joe, I'll still need your help with the costume.*

Yes, of course, said Joe, even fainter. *This really will be the last...*

The stage curtains opened on to a darkened stage. As light slowly brightened the gloom, the Ghost of Christmas Yet to Come seemed to emerge from the darkness itself. Its hooded form with outstretched hand took shape. There were audible gasps from the audience. No face was visible, but red eyes burnt beneath the hood. The boy who played Scrooge's dead body, lying on a filthy bed, trembled in fear. The hall grew colder still. Every eye was on that hooded figure, that outstretched hand, that hidden face that never uttered a word.

Scrooge looked upon his own death. He heard the scornful obituaries of those in the street, of those who scavenged for his few belongings. He saw Bob Cratchit kiss his dead child. He saw his own grave. Death and darkness all around him. Unless...

"I will honour Christmas in my heart," he cried. "And try to keep it all the year. I will live in the Past, the Present, and the Future. The Spirits of all three shall strive within me..."

He caught hold of James's outstretched hand. How icy it felt. A current seemed to pass into him before James pulled his hand away.

James faded back into the shadows, and slipped into the wings.

The applause was thunderous, but James did not go out again to take a bow.

Afterwards, the cast and some of the teachers crowded around him. They told him how brilliant he had been. How had he done it? How had he made his eyes glow red like that under the hood? How had he been so ghostlike? And where was that magnificent costume for the Ghost of Christmas Present? But James said nothing. Even when the headteacher came backstage to congratulate him, he kept quiet. He knew it was Joe's doing. Joe's last act.

The cast eventually melted away, to get changed, to meet their parents. Only Johnno and Mrs McNab lingered. Johnno whispered to him, "You'll tell me how you did it, won't you, James? You know I can keep a secret."

James smiled briefly, then nodded. "One day, Johnno, one day. When I'm ready. But not tonight." Johnno seemed satisfied with that.

"Well," said Mrs McNab. "Your mum and dad are going to be proud of you, James. That was a magnificent performance tonight." She rested her hands on his shoulders and searched his face. "What a remarkable boy you are. I expect you wish..." She was about to say, "I expect you wish that Joe had been here to see you," but she stopped herself. "Well, off you go, your parents will be waiting outside."

"Thank you, Mrs McNab," he said. "For everything."

James went into the cloakroom to be on his own for a minute or two.

Joe?

There was no answer.

Joe? he called again inside himself, more urgently.

No answer.

He listened to the silence inside him.

He could still feel Joe inside him, just, but as he stood there, in the silent, shadowy cloakroom, he understood why Joe was no longer answering. His voice was now Joe's, and Joe's was his. They were one. The Past, the Present, the Future, were all one now.

It was Sunday morning. Dad was already up. James was just coming from the bathroom in his pyjamas when Mum called him into his parents' bedroom.

He sat down on the bed beside her.

"I've been dreaming about your performance last night. It filled my head with such images. Do you know, I could have cried! It was so wonderful. You astounded your father..."

Briefly, he smiled. She saw he was preoccupied. "What's the matter, love?" she said softly. "It's not just because the play is over now, is it?"

But he shook his head. "I'm all right," he said. And he meant it.

She came to a sudden decision. Looking at him intently, she said, "James, I'm going to say something now which perhaps I shouldn't. It's been on my mind... I want you to answer me as truthfully as you can. It may sound strange..."

He looked up at her, seeming to understand what was coming. He gave her an encouraging nod.

"Some weeks ago I saw on the landing, well, what I thought was – was Joe. A ghost of Joe..."

She saw his eyes widen and a tremor pass over his shoulders.

"It was only for a few seconds... And I know I must have been mistaken."

But James shook his head, willing her to go on. She looked in wonder at the sudden relief on his face.

"And then, at the play, well, I felt him so near, up on the stage with you. I can't explain it. *Was he there, James?* Or am I not making sense?"

James straightened out and lay beside her, just as he used to when he was younger. There was a lump in his throat, but it was more from happiness than sadness. And then he smiled. "You weren't mistaken, Mum. He's been here all the time."

It was such a relief to tell her everything. He poured out the whole story, unable to stop himself. Finding Joe's ghost in the flats. Hearing Joe's voice in his head. Bringing his brother home. Taking him on trips with Zena and Johnno. Rehearsing at school. And then how they fell out. How Joe merged with him. How they were two halves, then gradually became one.

"He's part of me for ever, Mum. And I'm part of him. He's not dead, not really. He lives on inside me."

Mum had listened to him with her eyes closed, seeing everything so vividly as he told his story. She had no doubt that he spoke the truth. If she had not seen the ghost... If she had not seen the remarkable change in her son these last few weeks... If she had not seen gestures and heard phrases that reminded her of Joe... If she had not sat through those extraordinary apparitions on stage... She would have cried over this, cried for a son who could not let go, could not grieve. But she choked back the emotion. She leaned over him and saw the happiness in his eyes.

She hugged him tightly. After a while she said, "Don't say anything to your dad." They both laughed at the impossibility of that.

James did not hear Joe's voice again. But he wasn't quite sure that Joe had been entirely absorbed into his living body. At night he often had vivid dreams. He dreamt that he – or was it Joe? – rose out of his body like a ghost and floated through extraordinary worlds, vast spaces, flickering lights, stars. He carried those images with him throughout the day – his "spaced-out days" as Johnno took to calling them.

He's alive inside me, out there, in space, James said to himself. *Anywhere and everywhere.* And although Joe never spoke to him now, James continued to speak for them both.